C000122264

THE
LOVERS

ALSO BY YUMNA KASSAB

The House of Youssef
Australiana

THE
LOVERS

YUMNA KASSAB

ultimo
press

Published in 2022 by Ultimo Press,
an imprint of Hardie Grant Publishing

Ultimo Press
Gadigal Country
7, 45 Jones Street
Ultimo, NSW 2007
ultimopress.com.au

Ultimo Press (London)
5th & 6th Floors
52–54 Southwark Street
London SE1 1UN

All rights reserved. No part of this publication may be reproduced, stored in a retrieval system
or transmitted in any form by any means, electronic, mechanical, photocopying, recording
or otherwise, without the prior written permission of the publishers and copyright holders.

The moral rights of the author have been asserted.

Copyright © Yumna Kassab 2022

A catalogue record for this
book is available from the
National Library of Australia

The Lovers
ISBN 978 1 76115 062 3 (hardback)

Cover design Mika Tabata
Text design Bookhouse, Sydney
Typesetting Bookhouse, Sydney | 12/20 pt Sabon LT Pro
Copyeditor Ali Lavau
Proofreader Camha Pham

10 9 8 7 6 5 4 3 2 1

Printed in Australia by Griffin Press, an Accredited ISO AS/NZS 14001 Environmental
Management System printer.

The paper this book is printed on is certified against the
Forest Stewardship Council® Standards. Griffin Press holds
chain of custody certification SGSHK-COC-005088. FSC®
promotes environmentally responsible, socially beneficial and
economically viable management of the world's forests.

Ultimo Press acknowledges the Traditional Owners of the Country on which we work,
the Gadigal People of the Eora Nation and the Wurundjeri People of the Kulin Nation,
and recognises their continuing connection to the land, waters and culture.
We pay our respects to their Elders past and present.

FOR IBN BENITO ALMAGRO

Let fate have its hand

CONTENTS

BEGINNINGS 1

THE LETTERS 183

ENDINGS 207

BEGINNINGS

THE OPENING

What Amir loved most about Jamila was that she smelled of money. There was the perfume she used at her neck and wrists, there was the cream she rubbed into her skin, there was the shampoo that cost more than he made in a week. She was always in a gown that was from overseas and she would open it to him and say, 'Come to me.'

He could have died a happy man beneath her love, believing himself an entrant to Paradise at last but had she been local, chances are she would have been unworthy of a second glance. Amir knew this as he caressed her, he knew this as they joked about a future in which a child of theirs was born. They bantered over devotion and eternity but he knew if she found herself carrying a child, she would deal with it as efficiently as her gardener tended the perfect lawn.

Women like her did not stay, women like her only joked until it was time for her to return to her home. At best it was a dalliance, a sweet pleasure to enjoy until it dulled and then she could pack up her things and follow whatever light her circumstances offered her.

He watched her and wondered how much time was left to them. Was it a week, was it a month, would they see out the year together before she tied her robe again, and left him with a decaying memory of a fragrance that was hers? He told himself he would leave before pleasure turned to suffering, before their romance turned to ash, but he knew he would stay as long as Jamila would have him, as loyal as a servant, panting over her like any old dog.

DELUSION

I absolutely love this place. That is what Jamila said.

And what exactly do you love about it? Is it the building missing its ear or its side? Is it the electricity that only comes on in six-hour blocks? Is it that people must live with their parents because they have no other choice? Perhaps it is that we can't trust our government so it is left to us to limp along as best as we can? Is it the lawlessness of the roads, that obey no rules of reason or logic that can be deciphered by a rational mind? Is it that families do not speak to each other for generations over a slight you would take in your stride? Or perhaps it is that a university education is to no avail and in the end you will live a farmer's life?

The people are so much happier here.

You say this about the person who is begging in the streets because that is the only way they can get by. You say this about the refugee, the child of refugees who were also born to refugees, stretching all the way back to 1948. They live in shacks that have no water, no electricity, their possessions in bags because tomorrow the government may move them on. You say it about the daughter who has none but her family to fall back on, who leaves with only the clothes on her back—even her children belong to the husband—and there is nothing to say she has the right to ever see them again. She is not happy, she has no future, she smiles because it is a reflex and she has been taught her lines so well. You say this about the one who agonises in his bed and then passes on suddenly because no one knew how sick he was. He was not peaceful but his disease was undiagnosed so it had no name and therefore did not exist.

I sense so much possibility.

You sense it because you are used to another life. You have money but will you sense possibility when your money runs out? Even if it does run out, you can take your suitcase, fill it with your things and return to that other country, and you can trust that between fortune and your government, the conditions are provided so you will prosper again. There is no possibility here, only that forced by people with their bare hands. The truth is we live like this because we have no choice, and if given a choice, we would choose to live our lives according to the pattern you live by overseas.

RAGE

Jamila was at breakfast. Her mother and aunt sat opposite her and they broke the conversation to have a bite. It was a temporary ceasefire and now was the time to regroup her troops. Her best defence was silence and to avoid their eyes. If her eyes met theirs, they would sense her uncertainty and redouble their attacks. It did not matter how many times they did this. Each time it was the house of cement collapsing on her head.

A woman with your possibilities, with your education, your wealth should not lower herself like this.

You could have your pick of men and you choose Amir who steals into your room in the night.

Don't kid yourself. He comes for your money, not your love.

And then the variations on this, tiny words changed, the order mixed up, their artillery launched onto her plate.

Lucy came in with a tray—milk, bread, fruit—and she had added rose petals because that was what Jamila had taught her to do.

She distributed the contents of the tray and then left, humming as she went.

Lucy herself had a love back home and when the time was right, she would let her family know. It would be simple, Lucy explained. The boyfriend was saving, together they would get a place, have some children, what more could we want?

Jamila thought of Amir, of how she used every weapon in the book to make him believe their love had a future, that—world aside—they had a hope.

Most nights he nodded his agreement, not because they were on the same page, but to keep the peace. She had the rage of a dragon. It made him fearful, it made him come alive. He kissed her and said, 'Be at peace. We still have the night.'

Her mother poured milk in the tea even though Jamila had repeatedly said she did not want milk in her tea. Jamila grabbed the tray and launched it out the window and waited for the crash. Then there was their silence and she decided it was time for a quiet cigarette outside.

FREEDOM

Once Jamila had believed that if she left, she would be free at last. So she left but she carried the stupidity of their world inside her.

Once she believed if she had enough money, they would leave her alone but no matter how high she built the fortress walls, they were family and they wormed their way in with a trick and a plea.

Once she believed she could move across the world and there at last she would be left alone. Alas, they followed her and said, 'Did you think you'd get away so easily?'

Once she believed in freedom but now it sits in a disused box. Not the United Nations, not the president, God or all the King's men had the power to intercede on her behalf.

ATTRACTION

Amir was not an attractive man. Even Jamila said it. And then she whispered, 'But I love you all the same.'

He thought of saying something that would shut her up, that would silence her for the rest of time.

Your ears stick out. A dentist could help you with your smile.

The words were on his tongue. They would have slipped out if it weren't for his restraint.

Anything he said would wound her ten times more than the words he'd heard from her. It was likely she wouldn't forgive him, that she would walk out. And perhaps the drama, the excitement, would be satisfying for a minute, but the effort to win her back would be too great.

So he touched her hair and said soft things.

He soothed her every night.

He counted her fury as charming, he made note of every time she laughed.

He called her beautiful and incredible and he felt her quieten at his side.

When she said to him, 'Without you there is no light in my life,' he thought, *But when you leave, I know I will want them to bury me alive.*

Better a thought than words where they would torment him, and her, robbing them of the flavour their time together still had.

PLAY

Samir invited the boys around for cards and they played till after one. He regretted that his partner was Mohammed who was the weakest player and together they lost round after round.

The night was getting on and Amir wondered about Jamila home alone. He thought about the wife he'd once had and the varieties of failure the universe can provide. Their families had smiled upon their marriage but if they had lived on an upper floor, he would have thrown his wife off the balcony.

Lucky there were no children. Lucky. Even these three friends said it. Some relationships are fated. Others operate outside the universe's control.

Mohammed lost them another round and Amir excused himself to go outside. When his wife went screaming to her parents' house, his mother said, 'You need to go get her. Her life is at your side.'

Why was it that she offered this advice so easily when it tripped him as if his ankles were tied? Amir retrieved her like a pet, like a suitcase, like a car that had been misplaced. She came willingly but that night, the boys knew better than to ask about his wife. Even their women had stayed away and avoided his eyes.

He remembered when the marriage was done how he played at Samir's house till the sun came up, how he smoked so heavily he couldn't breathe, how he cleared every memory of her until there was no evidence that once upon a time a wife walked on this floor.

Another wife, his mother urged, but the thought sickened him and he imagined a lifetime ahead—alone— and how in such solitude there would be satisfaction of a peaceful kind.

Samir was the one who called it a night, who told them it was time they went to their beds, that they could come around tomorrow at the same time again.

As he was leaving, Samir stood close to him and said, 'It's good to see you looking alive once more.'

He thought of those words as he drove away and he thought of visiting Jamila so late. He could walk through the gate that squeaked, that was a dead giveaway for the neighbour who spied.

It did not take him long to make up his mind and turn the car so that he would be with her when the sun next showed its face.

She was asleep when he arrived but she woke and patted the bed at her side. 'Where have you been this night?'

She welcomed him beneath the sheets and when she whispered in his ear, he smiled and thought, *This is paradise.*

NEUTRALITY

Capitalism is not bad. It depends how it's implemented. Communism is good, in theory, but people mess it up.

A nuclear bomb is neutral. It comes down to how it is used.

Their sentences floated over her head. They chased her down the hall. She ate them with her breakfast. She took them into the shower and pretended they weren't acidic as she bathed.

Sometimes she cried. Sometimes. Mostly she was silent. Mostly she stayed inside.

These words on the TV, these were the words in the books. Her head was a dreamcatcher pulling them to tangle inside her whenever she went outside. Lately she goes between people who say that religion is not all doom and gloom.

Religion is like a political system. Any issues are related to its misuse.

Jamila thought of her father beating her mother nightly. *It is written. It is my right as a man.*

She thought of women as the greatest soldiers of war, more than those who were on the frontline.

She saw the women she knew cooling their heels, then settling down to whatever life dished their way.

She considered the weight of fabric, considered the endless justification of history.

It is called peace but the truth is we are more often asked to submit.

Peace. Submission.

Pick or choose.

Her mother said this as she put a patch over an injured eye. *He is not a monster. Do not blame the crimes of man on our religion, which really means peace.*

Every night she dreams. It is inevitable, no?

They chase her, they drag her by her hair, by her feet, by whatever part of her they can reach. They laugh as they destroy her. *It is destiny. We are mere agents delivering on truth.*

It is a nightmare, it is a nightmare, she dreams and dreams, and even when she wakes, she knows she has not escaped.

PEACE

Amir stood on the edge of the mountain. Amazing. This mountain had stood over every day of his life and he had not noticed it before. It surprised him to consider an alternative life in which this mountain did not exist. Say he looked to the east—his eyes could see into the horizon—and for as long as he could remember, this mountain has been the companion to his hopes and dreams.

When he was younger, his parents talked about taking the car and making a trip of it. A caravan of cars, out for the day, breakfast, lunch and snacks so that they could find a spot on the side of the road and then spread out.

Someday, someday, and he had grown up and it had taken till he was a man possessed to abandon the day and head up to see what the mountain had to say.

The place he stands is rocky, the ground is unstable, but he has no recklessness in his heart. Jamila is the reckless one, the one who may drive her car off a cliff, who may take her grandmother's only cups and smash them on the floor. That is her style, not his, but she gave him the keys and said, 'Go for a drive.'

Go for a drive and there is so much to do.

Go for a drive, solitary, when I could be with you.

Go for a drive without knowing how the journey ends or even if it begins.

He brought nothing to drink, nothing to eat. This was an hour stolen away but standing alone, the sea blue as far as the eye could reach, he understood at last that his heart was at peace.

He wondered at Jamila trusting him with the car that was her pride and joy. It was the only one of its kind in the country and it was better suited to arriving at nightclubs than a trip to the mountainside. Over every bump he winced as the dust kicked up, he worried over how he would wash it before returning it to her. But for now he stood and breathed and when the hour was up, he went back to the car and drove leisurely down. In their town, people came out to watch, they noted who was at the wheel. He did not beep a hello, he did not wind down the window to wave and chat. He did not want to attract any more notice than he already had.

When he arrived at her place, she was sitting in the sun, her hair curled, her nails freshly done. She smiled at him as he arrived, she blew a kiss and waited for him to park. He came over to her, a thousand apologies on his tongue for the state of the car. He had rehearsed the sentences and the words needed only to be said.

Before he could speak, she pulled him to her—she was always like the sun—and said *I hope you enjoyed yourself* and after that, he couldn't remember what he'd meant to say.

TORMENT

Amir meant to love her. It was his intent. He would love her completely, he would love her like summer air. Everything he had would be hers on a platter and tell me, what is nicer than the ability to serve?

He brought his wife home like a treasure, he unwrapped her like a gift on their bed. He kissed her hair, he kissed her hands, he marvelled at her from night till dawn and then for the hours beyond.

If there was a lesson, it was that their love was not his alone. He could shower her with his love as if it were all the gold of the world, he could build her a palace with his bare hands but his love was not shared and like a puddle of water, given time, it would evaporate.

His great love was met with a war.

His affection was met with a bite.

His desire to serve her was mocked.

Her words were like weapons and down they rained, and he told himself he was unsurprised but the truth was their fights had not been in his plans. He kept away, he avoided her eyes, he steered clear of the room she was in, and he began to pray.

He asks himself why he resorted to prayer at such a time, he who had learned the rituals but never prayed genuinely in his life? With his prayers was the hope they go their separate ways, he on an alternative path, she to whatever lay in wait. The world was filled with examples of great love being extinguished by an anvil called circumstance or chaos, depending on your frame of mind. It was possible this would not be the rest of his life.

He extracted himself as best as he could but where there's breakage, there's damage, and although time heals, he knew he'd always bear her memory as a trace. She left without a goodbye and he believed he could now begin his separate life.

People urged him to women again, that relationships were prescribed as much as the setting of the sun, but he was spent, he was emptied, and he did not believe he could love again until he met Jamila in the summertime.

Some call it destiny but it does not matter how it is named. It had the feeling of ease, it had the weight of fate and it was a love only the heavens could have arranged.

MY LOVE SO YOUNG

Religion should not be transactional. *Dear God, give me this and I will obey. Dear God, I need an extra suit because this one is worn and in return I will pray double time this week.* He knows it is not meant to be like that but he finds himself praying and Amir wishes he could have known Jamila when she was young, before her face was lined and she touches the white in her hair and laughs, waiting for him to say it adds to her beauty anyway.

I want to have known her when she was young so I can understand.

He wonders what he will have to pay for the granting of this wish but never mind, they are both alive and she is so young but it is still her, make no mistake. The only difference is she smiles more and age has not yet begun to soften her shoulders and make them round.

He watches her and then raises a hand and calls out her name.

She stops. He is a stranger. She will not know him for another life.

He wants to say something to her, to tell her he understands, that she is the only one he will truly love but he is cautious about forcing the hand of fate, how a slight tinkering could alter the course of their lives.

She waits for him and he says *I am sorry, I thought you were someone else*. She continues on her way, his love so young, and he returns to his home and thinks *I am the luckiest man fate has played with since the start of time*.

SHARK DREAMS

Lately a shark disturbs her dreams.

She is by the sea and she is standing on the shore with her dress hitched above her knees. She wades in, holding her dress, watching the roughness of the surf, wondering why she doesn't go home. It would be easy. Walk home, change her clothes, then warm her toes, but she finds herself shivering, asking if this is the day she will drown, the day that danger edges closer to threaten her.

The waves buffet her and she releases her dress. It is pointless to hold it. In these conditions, she is going to get wet and she should be prepared to stand unprotected before the grey terror of this wintry world.

She has heard a rumour about a shark and she knows better than to believe a shark can be tamed, that she can do anything except tend it briefly, release it and hope she doesn't lose her nose or a toe.

She finds the shark lying like a dead fish on its side. Chances are it has already expired. She is weighed by her dress but she tries to use it to her advantage, tying it to the shark's tail and tugging it back to shore.

What does a shark need so it doesn't suffocate before the fireplace? She bathes it with warm water, she sings it a song, she calls it to breathe and take to life. Days of no response and she senses the futility of her actions. She promises she will only keep it one more day before she buries it outside but she can't bear to do so, not when she has run her hand over its body, not when so many nights she has cried.

She arranges the burial, she takes the shark outside. She wraps it in the dress that was a sign of the time she hoped before life proved her hope a lie.

THE LOVERS

She tells herself to begin, that the shark is dead, but she can't bury it so she leaves it in the grave she's made and walks away.

Always she wakes to a knock at the door and it is her love, carrying her dress and asking to be allowed again the warmth of the fireplace.

SILENCE

The greater the water she pours, the greater his emptiness seems. She had thought by now he would have been filled to the brim, that there would be a break but instead his demands grow and she now believes them to be without end.

He cannot satisfy her, he will never satisfy her, he should have left Jamila to other men.

He compares his ankle with hers and he wonders how such a small-footed creature could cause him so much pain. He holds up her hand, he envelops it in his own, and he wonders how defeat can be exacted with her as the tiniest dose. He stands by her—he hovers actually—and he is uncertain before her other men. He asks her about them and she offers them like pearls that will make him choke. Her transparency, her ease, these he counts as qualities he loves, but about her past, he wishes she weren't so free. He wishes she kept the details to herself, that she did not have this crushing capacity to share.

What can he give her, what can he offer, what can he do to make her promise to stay at his side for the rest of their lives? What is there? Is there his lack of money, is there his absence of knowledge about the world, is he to keep her with his ordinariness (because, let us be honest, she has her choice of men)? What is there? Are there the details of his past? Is there his family which is more dysfunctional than most? But here she disagrees. His family is no worse, no better than her own.

He wakes in the middle of the night and she asks him where he is going. He kisses her before leaving quietly into the night, thinking about the life he knew, the life that awaits, how he never outgrew his uncertainty. He has carried it with him and he is unsure how to shed this solitude that is more comfortable than a home. How is he to do this? How is he to leave his past behind so he can meet her somewhere to give her the kindness that she deserves?

There is him, there is the night, there are his questions and his only answer is the silence all around.

PLEASURE

He emerges from her bedroom, he knows not to what world. Hours he has drowned and it all started with her saying, 'Come, my sailor, let the captain teach you a lesson in ownership.'

Amir has heard stories of men driven mad by women, a woman taking complete possession and then refusing to release her hold, and he called such men crazy, inhabitants of the imaginary, creatures as unreal as fairytales told to children at night.

She whispers something in his ear, and he wonders if it is a dare, a challenge, a promise or all of the above?

He is afraid that these pieces will break asunder and he will be like Humpty Dumpty in the nursery rhyme. He will not worry. That is a trouble for another night. Instead he goes to sleep smiling, and he thinks of pleasure, its texture, how it is desire bringing love to life.

FEATHERS

It had been another night of cards. Samir served them their drinks, the ashtray on the table was clean, and there were the small snacks they didn't notice themselves eating. They kept a tally of winners and losers, the playing pairs to which they belonged, but they played for so many hours that he threw down his cards and yawned and said he was slowly going blind.

They laughed and said it was as good a time as any to have a break. Samir's children filtered through, swapping glasses, emptying the ash tray, and he asked them what else they had in the fridge, if there was something other than coffee and tea. He poured them soft drinks, they all agreed it was getting late, and Samir said that before they went he had a story for them.

And so the story went.

'Once—this was years ago—there was a farmer who wanted to keep a bird. He put together all the money he had and went to the market and bought himself the most beautiful bird. It came with a big cage and the seller told him if he fed the bird apples, it would begin to speak. "That is how I've trained her but I make no promises because she is unreliable like all the daughters of Eve." So the farmer took his bird home and he praised its colours day and night. He occasionally let her out, he had this fantasy she was a rich princess and one day she would let her song be heard. He fed her as many apples as he could afford but that bird never said a single word, so he became angry that he had been taken for a ride and all he had was this ordinary bird. Mind you, it had the most glorious colours and the seller made a point that the bird might not sing. The farmer knew deep down he had bought the bird for her colours rather than her words but if you see the same colours every day, you tire of them, and suddenly you want to hear some words. He thought, *I have given her apples and now I shall ignore her and she can starve in her cage for all I care*, but he had the sense to leave the door open because he did not want her death on his conscience. He reasoned that he could explain to God her escape had been an accident, if a misfortune later befell the bird. And of course there was a misfortune. The bird became more and more miserable, she shrunk into herself and finally lost her feathers. The farmer was so furious he took the cage outside and he hoped to God that in the morning he'd wake and find he was rid of so miserable a bird. He got his wish in a way. The next morning, there was a woman frozen at the door of the cage, and he knew she had been the bird. So he did what we're all meant to do: he carried her to a quiet place and buried her in the ground, wondering why he couldn't be content with feathers, why he had also demanded the song. If only, if only . . . but this is an old story. The world giving you feathers, the feathers you prayed for, and then you discover what you really want is a song.'

They were silent for a second and then they made jokes about Samir and his story. 'Tell us more about the feathers of the bird.' 'You can play cards, you can even serve coffee but yours are the stupidest stories I have ever heard.'

Samir said nothing but the next night there were no jokes about birds, women, feathers, storytelling or anything else. Jouad's missing wife had been found in a neighbouring village and it was said she had been starved to death.

Samir let them play a round and then he said he needed to go to bed. They left silently and wondered about the stories, how fact and fiction both use the same words.

The previous night he went to visit Jamila. He had expected her to be home but she wasn't. When he spoke to her in the morning, she said she had been out with friends. She volunteered no other details and he thought no more of it until Jouad was found beaten so badly that his mother was inconsolable when she saw her son's face. It was nothing, he told himself, but casually one time he asked her what had happened to the baseball bat she kept by the fireplace.

'Some kids borrowed it. Who knows? Maybe one day it will be returned.'

Eventually Samir had them around again for cards and they stuck to games except when Samir was in the mood to tell them a story. Amir came to hate the stories, bracing himself for what he was about to hear, but he told himself they were only stories, to tolerate them, *push them from your mind*, and that was what he told himself each night so that he was peaceful enough to sleep.

SHAME

PART I

He wonders where Jamila's going with this, if this is an instance of letting a storm wear itself out . . .

'The first boy I loved, properly loved, did not care for me the same. I was driven to desperation and you would not believe the lengths I was driven to, how badly I wanted to impress, how I wanted him to want me above everything else in the world, but in the end, I couldn't make him or any of the others stay. Every single love died and I wondered if it was worth the heartache and the pain.'

'I dressed for him, I danced for him, I plucked myself till I was bare and there was nothing else I could do.

'Before I slept with him, I slept with someone else, learning tricks, wanting to torture him slowly on that bed but what was any of it really worth? It makes me sad to think of myself, so young, so full of desire, and how all I wanted was for someone with a bit of attention to spare.'

'This story repeated itself so many times till I was sick with the weariness of it, with these romantic defeats. I wanted no more, I wanted to wash my hands, to say enough is enough, but it is a game I like and I find myself returning again and again, stepping in to play. Would I change it, would I change what I did, who I pursued, who I allowed into my life? I find it hard to regret my life in this way. Yes, there was much pain, yes, I wanted to die, but at least I tried, I loved, and it made me feel so alive.'

'I wanted to tell you this. I wanted you to understand. For once in my life, I wanted to be motivated by promise rather than worry that the one I care for means to escape. I know I cannot make anyone stay. I know this. We all know this but tell me how much of what we do is logic and reason, how much is persistence in the face of contradictory evidence?'

'This is the first time I have told anyone this, this is the first time I have let my guard down in this way. It makes me fear where we might go from here but if I don't do this now, when will I do it? Do I grow older, older, hiding because of my very human fears?'

PART II

She wonders where Amir is going with this, if he will exhaust himself given enough time . . .

'I gave her everything. I would have given her my life if I could and all I wanted was something small, a nice word, occasionally a smile, but she was like a storm, constant, and there was no calming her down. It hurts later when people say *I told you so*, when they say that you shouldn't have wasted your time, that you were trying to give breath to a dead animal that cannot be brought back to life. What help is that to me? What good does it do for me to be reminded of this? Really I loved her and all the love in the world was not enough to make her smile just once in the morning and once before she slept in the night.'

'I told myself I will be this good person, I will be a good man, I will not be like those who seek to control the woman in their life but her behaviour honestly drove me near out of my mind. I couldn't eat, I couldn't sleep and I knew that nothing, absolutely nothing, would be enough.'

'I had this fear that another man would come along and she would run off with him. It was completely unjustified.

She was many things but she was not the type to play around. Still I couldn't shake this fear, and I thought, I will get my kicks while I can, I will have a woman on the side, and I went so far as to look around, but Samir, he pulled me aside and said, "If you can't love her properly, if she does not feel the same, then it is better each person goes their way, that you don't force yourself through a torture when you can have peace of a different kind."'

'We have gone far, we have come close, what is there that remains to be said? These hurts of the past will not protect us from the future, they will not protect us from being hurt again but we go forth in life, we dance as best as we can. This is the bargain we accept and it follows us from our birth till we breathe our very last breath.'

POSSIBILITY

Jamila considers the people around her. There is the family nearby, eating quickly as if in a race. There is the pair, a young couple, away from parental eyes for a moment. She remembers times like this when she stole away, how she still steals away, how her lover is a shadow in her life, how she denies the presence of permanency.

What happens once we become used to each other, once we become bored, once we anticipate each other's moods like the seasons cycled in a day? What happens when you are tired of me and I tire of you? What keeps us together except the routine of a child and the boundaries of marriage and the law?

She considers the waiter, a man in his fifties who places bread on each table, who fills up each cup until it almost overflows. In the time she has frequented this breakfast place, he has always been here. She does not believe he takes a day off. She wonders if he has a wife, children, and it is likely. She imagines them warming themselves in the evening by a fire. He probably starts at 6, giving him an hour to prepare before the first customers appear, then finishing at midday when the doors shut for the day.

There is an old woman alone. Her hair is uncovered and she wears four necklaces over her jacket. Jamila has seen this woman so many times they often say hello.

Jamila has come with Amir on the days he does not work but she tends to frequent this place alone. It is a ten-minute drive and the food is always the same. Her aunt reprimands her: the wastefulness of having breakfast out when you can eat as well at home, and she shrugs because we take nothing into the next life except our bodies and the weight of what we did with our life.

She asks for another coffee. The waiter serves her with a smile, he asks after her plans for the day and she gives him a vague answer, one that satisfies his question but gives nothing away.

She drinks this coffee slowly. She thinks about the day ahead, she thinks about the night with him that has passed. She studies the family and imagines herself breakfasting with him in this way, a child of theirs at her side or his, or maybe one each for them to tend to, to drive them up the wall. She considers it, wondering about the longevity of such a fantasy, if it will have any life beyond a day, if it won't be strained, if subjecting it to the regular strains of life wouldn't ultimately break the camel's back of love. She wonders if it's worth the risk, if the storms that arise will be storms weathered, if they can see them to the other side. Why can't we stay happy like this? Why is it the human condition to seek the greenness of spaces outside our current life?

She considers and her mind makes its turn. She wonders about discussing it with him, the one who insists repeatedly that she commit to a future, to know he wants to spend the future at her side.

THE LUXURY OF SUICIDE

Here suicide is a quiet thing. There is no drama, there is no outward yell. It is the sigh trapped inside that has been forgotten by the world.

Amir considers it. There is the one who swallowed poison and climbed into bed to die. There is the one who drove the truck off the cliff. The family insist it was an accident. There is the gun, the rope, the chair. There is the romantic version—Hollywood—where the mourners gather and they are allowed the solace of tears, and he considers the days of darkness that have been his, how he never considered jumping off a bridge, falling to the rocks at the edge of a polluted sea. He could lie down on the train tracks but the train has long since stopped running, and the fuel required to set himself on fire is fuel needed to keep his family alive.

When she lent him her car, he considered again the subject of suicide. It would be romantic, it would be a statement to the world, but he was in another place now and besides, the car was hers, not his, and the last thing he wanted was to inconvenience the one he loved who told him daily that she loved him too.

THE BOYFRIENDS

Um Bilal, we remembered her as a girl of fifteen even though she is well into her forties. We heard about that marriage overseas, the one that did not work out, and how a lesser woman would have retreated from life and waited to die, but eventually she returned here, and she brought with her a son, a boy of four or five, and she gave the vaguest answers about who had fathered him. We all asked but she never said anything that satisfied our curiosity. She lived with that boy alone above the bakery, and from that time she received men into her bed. Some said she did it for money, others said it was to battle the loneliness of the nights, others still that she was a light woman, not much upstairs, or else she would see how people called her every name under the sun, that when they were particularly spiteful, claws out and swiping, they said them to her face and even to her son. This son was not Bilal but another and I know for a fact that Bilal lived with his father overseas and you know how you sit in the night, the fire is low and the tongue a little loose, and we would wonder—all of us did—what sort of mother leaves her son overseas and then is able to hold her head up and speak normally to strangers in the street?

She left her son overseas.

The men, one leaves and then another takes his place, and don't believe for a second when they say they're her friends. Women and men, they cannot be friends, and it is better for them to make friends from among their own sex.

She has never become rich but her money over the years has stayed the same even as the country has declined. For a brief period, they say she stays alone, she bides her time, the wind will turn and then she will be visited day and night again. I always remember her at fifteen or as she is in recent years: in a bathrobe, her hair in curlers, her feet propped up on the balcony. She wears slippers and she shows their soles to the world. Her son is grown and he has children of his own and he visits his mother daily, he brings her fruit, he brings her plates of food that his wife has cooked, and I heard the other day that maybe she no longer receives men because she's done using them, that she has no need anymore for them, that her son is all grown and he is taller than the men around him who look up to him from within his shadow, that he can now support her as she ages, that if she wants she can retreat from the world, she can hide and watch television all day and paint her nails in the sun as a woman of leisure as all women hope to be but come now, the mind is tired and the fire burns low so let us turn to our own lives, their failures, their hopes, and how no matter the stakes, we bear the darkness willingly because God promises us in the morning it will be light again.

NOCTURNES

She is calling the one she loves.

There. It is out in the world.

She lets the phone ring.

She is armed with an excuse, a reason for the call. I need to check the homework for maths. Truth be told, people call her to check but he does not know that.

That first love, how they snuck around. The illicit catch-ups, their meetings carefully arranged: the notes passed, the plotting and planning as if they were complex strategists and the fate of the world was at stake.

She thinks of the girl she had been and her profound silliness and how she is sneaking around with him.

Amir visits her bed and then he leaves. Everyone knows it but none dare speak of it. To speak of it is to take it out of the night-time and air it in daylight, to legitimise it, to give it life, to say to the world *I may well be serious about this one*, to subject their young love to scrutiny, to comparisons, to turn it into a house of glass for the stones others throw with indifference or intent. She could not bear that, not at this early stage.

He asks her to marry him and she resists. She tells him he is joking, that he can't be serious, and he repeats he means the words that he has said.

She thinks of marriage, she thinks of being bolted to the ground, of being stuck to the floor, and she tells herself that with him it will be different but isn't that the line everyone the world over feeds to their self? He calls it her western cynicism, that with him there is no need for a mask, that he wants her in his life, that he will not let her go, that he does not care what anyone thinks.

That is how it always starts, she mutters and thinks of how hopeful she has been, rolling up her sleeves to greet each beginning with hope and how each time it had been cut down, of how many loves have died despite all her energy, her will and intent.

And what is there except a hope that this one will not go the way of the others and die a premature death?

It is a hope, nothing else. Upon it, the world turns, the axis of the globe, its tilt, and she wonders if she is willing to enter the ring again, to stake it all on a hope, a promise of something else but as he said to her: *Tell me, is there anything else?*

DUTY

The doubts are the worst.

Amal is telling her story—*he hit me just then*—and all Jamila can think is *here we go again*.

The doubts?

There are no bruises, Amal always has a smile on her face. If things are so bad, why hasn't she left? Surely it's not as she says. Come on, there is the door and no one is standing in her way.

But as a good friend, she listens, she nods often, she does not roll her eyes. As a good friend, she offers tea and biscuits, she offers tissues—here come the tears

YUMNA KASSAB

like clockwork—and she agrees that he is to blame for Amal's pain.

It takes an hour to calm her, to farewell her, to breathe a sigh of relief, ignoring the fact that in a week they will be revisiting the same mess that is the soundtrack of Amal's marriage. She is grateful it is someone else's lot in life, that she can wash her hands of it and consider her social duty discharged, making a decision about how to do her hair and the clothes she wants to wear.

She has tossed and turned over this subject at night. *How can I be a better friend? What else can I do to help her other than offer bandaids and painkillers after the beast has whipped her again?*

It is not my place, she tells her reflection, *she must sleep in the bed she has made, didn't she choose to marry him when we all shook our heads?*

What else can I do? she wonders, transferring a pin from her mouth into her hair, *I offer her shelter every time, I listen to her, I give her advice, I remind her how to make her life bearable, but the horse has been led to water and I can offer nothing else.*

72

She does the same thing after each one of Amal's visits. She goes around with some treats and toys for the kids. She asks Amal if she's okay and her friend nods emphatically *yes, yes!* She is always grateful for that *yes, yes* which absolves her, dismisses her and allows her to return home to think about what else remains on her list for the day. And it could continue like this—their arrangement—except he goes too far and Amal never shows up again.

DISCOURSE

Samir was in one of his moods. He was ready to talk. It had been a long night and once his tongue was loosened, Amir knew the night had more hours remaining in it than had been left behind.

He started with 'The King and the Slave', a story they had all heard before.

'Once upon a time long ago, there was a king who had thousands of slaves. The slaves were blue and green, red, pink and white. They were every colour that existed under the sun. The king had slaves to arrange his pillows, slaves to tie his shoes, slaves to polish his mobile phone, slaves to spin silk so that, if the fancy took him, he could order silk socks in every colour while he drank champagne and complained about his weight.

'His slaves conspired in the only way slaves can, turning foolish fantasies, thinking *one day, one day* when men, let us be clear, they had as great a chance at freedom as another man has of spending a night between my wife's legs. They could plot as much as they liked, they could dare to look at the palace's walls but tell me, how did they mean to survive outside when they did not even own the scraps they slept in at night? They had never been outside and they knew zero about the world and some of them believed there was no other world, that the entire world was what was contained within the palace walls. And in a sense they were right because the palace was the world in miniature, with all its suffering and stupidity, its fighting and fantasies, and if they needed to study the world, they need only look around them.

'But there was a slave who dreamed of freedom. Of course there was such a slave or else our story has nowhere to go. We shall call him Zaki and this name suits him more than the one his parents could provide.

'As a young man, he thought about the world outside, he studied the paintings and photographs in the palace for clues by which to understand the world he had never seen in his life. Ah, it is easy for me and you to make our plans but what if your life is reduced like Zaki's, how would you even begin to imagine an escape? Your parents tell stories of slavery as their parents told them—in this fashion all the way back—so that no other life ever existed, and no other future exists except more of the same.

'He looked in books, at the pictures, he was alert to what the messengers brought in their news, he watched the merchants who brought goods to the gates and often he was one of the slaves sent to retrieve the crates but they were never allowed when the gates were open because our king is wise and knew better than to permit the enslaved a glimpse outside. Our king is wise—of course he is—because if he was the stupidest man, he would have been educated till his head was as stuffed as his belly, even then if he showed signs of ineptitude, his advisers would save his royal grace so he'd be counted the wisest of men, the best, the greatest, the grandest and the other words attached to royalty from their birth.

'Let us consider Zaki's options. If he made a run for it, he would be gunned down. He could attempt to sneak out but believe me, there were no holes in the walls he had studied his entire life. He could smuggle himself out like a parcel in a cart of weapons and he supposed that was his best chance. And that is what he did. He lay down in the cart, he did not dare breathe, he had no plans beyond his escape. The cart moved, he had no way of guessing how far he had travelled. He was in so much darkness because of the covering, it may as well have been the darkness of a night.

'The cart stopped and the covering removed and tonight I am in a good mood, I sit with my friends, so our slave jumps up like this'—Samir demonstrates, almost knocking the card table with his feet—'and he gets away and he is free just like you and me till the end of his days.

'But we are realists and despite our good diet of optimism and dreams and God on our side, the chances of Zaki finding his freedom are so tiny they may as well not exist. Say they catch him and they drag him back to the palace by his hair and his feet, his leg is chopped at the knee so he cannot repeat the offence. Say he makes his dash for freedom and he escapes but his only life is begging on the streets. You know, this is the likeliest outcome for Zaki and so while he is a free man he will be forever denied the pittance we use to keep poverty at bay, those morsels we have in our reach. Say he escapes and he finds fortune, maybe he finds a gold coin and that is his start but the elephants will fly and my name would not be Samir and I would chop the ends of my moustache and put on a woman's clothes so that everyone knows how wrong I've been, but I won't be wrong: Zaki probably dies and his chances of surviving—a proper free man—are so miserable he may as well resign himself to his lot in life.'

One of them throws a peanut at Samir. Another tells him to focus on his cards because he had lost another hand, but later I took his story, it kept me up at night, and I imagined Zaki in his bid for freedom, and I dreamed he finally escaped, he sat in the sun, he played cards with his friends, he had kids and a wife, and in the morning I wake in tears, unsure if it was because of my dream or if it was Samir's words that continued to play on my mind.

FACTS

'I am going to see Abu Khalil about some work.'

'There are other ways to sell your soul and they won't cost you so much.'

'The future is on my mind. There is a change I want in my life and I need more money than I currently have.'

'Is this about her?'

'No, not just that,' I lied. He knew the truth anyway.

'Work harder in the job you have.'

'I can only make so much that way.'

'I want to tell you money doesn't matter but of course it does and anyhow, if you're thinking like this, no matter how much money you have it will never be enough.'

'It's not like that. I know the situation. I tell myself that if she was after money, she would go for someone else. I console myself with this but . . .'

'If she's going to leave, no amount of money is going to make her stay.'

'I know that.'

'But do you understand that you are powerless, that this is out of your hands? Have you resigned yourself to the facts?'

'And what are the facts?'

'She will always be richer, she will always belong to another world that is different to the one that is your home. If you can make a life together like this, so be it but if you cannot, you won't be the first to fail.'

I wished he'd add some sweetness to his words.

He looked at me. We were face to face. 'You are my friend and you have always been like a brother to me. The thing you want is the thing I once wished I had. If it weren't for her, we would not be having this conversation in the first place. You would not be telling me you are going to sell your soul to be in the service of the fattest rat there is in this town. I know the lure of money. We want more to fill our eyes but if you do this, you will lose your sleep, you will lose your peace and you will lose any chance at a life with the one you wish to keep at your side. She will not recognise you. You will not be worth looking at twice. As you make your calculations, do not forget to include this in your tally as well. You remain poor, you keep your hands clean or you gather your riches and forever there will be emptiness in your life.'

He offered me a cigarette and I took it and I did the same with the next ten after as he first did when we were twelve. When he said my hands were shaking, I said it was the combination of coffee and cigarettes. He smiled and left it at that.

FIGHTING

Lubna said to her, *It is all right, I will go into the store alone.* With that, she marched in without checking if Jamila was coming in or staying outside.

She trailed after Lubna who was already arguing with the owner of the store. The dress was laid between them, a territorial dispute, and she could hear both their voices rising: Lubna yelling that the dress was not of the quality promised, look here at the stitching, the looseness of the threads . . . and the owner shaking his head and saying you have done this before, trying to return a dress you have already worn.

She stayed where she was, smoking a cigarette in the doorway, trying to blow the smoke outside. She listened to their voices and each time she thought they were reaching an agreement, they gridlocked and the argument continued on.

Lubna had in fact worn the dress. She had worn it last night to the wedding and when she'd been asked how she could afford such a dress (*They can't afford to eat* was whispered), she merely smiled and said she had her ways.

Lubna explained the situation on the way into town. *Really, I have only borrowed the dress. It is as good as when I bought it yesterday. Put it next to a new one and, trust me, you can't tell the difference between the two.*

Hence the trip, hence the argument, hence Jamila wondering if this argument would ever end. She considered walking in and offering quietly to buy it, but later when she'd tell him about her day, about the dress and how she'd bought it, he'd shake his head and say, *This is one more instance when you think your money will solve the problems of the world.*

It wasn't like that. It was a simple solution. Everyone would be happy. Everyone could walk away, assuming that is what Lubna wanted in the first place. *Everyone can walk away if they have money, everyone can make the choices I make if they had the money I have.* She imagines telling him this and to prove her imaginary point, she almost walks in and pays for the dress but instead she walks away because she can. As for Lubna, even if she could walk away, she would not, but that was not Jamila's problem anyway.

LIES

She lied. They all lied. She consoled herself with this.

She was less guilty because other people were guiltier. Guilt was not decided in isolation. Guilt was relative and so she lied and so did they but she lied less than them.

She told him she was on a break. A break from work, a break from life. The break stretched from the expected month and she had been here almost a year and she made no plans yet to leave.

She did not want to leave him. She did not want to bring him with her. She worried that if she returned to her life, she returned to her pain and it would break the both of them, and so she sheltered here on a permanent holiday, keeping her head down so no one would ask after her plans. She had this sense—stupid, she knew—that someone was going to call up and ask her to explain herself. *What are your plans, when do you plan to leave, why aren't you working?*

She would protest, she would defend, she would lie some more, she went through these days expecting always to be exposed. The truth would be laid bare. She stayed because she had nothing else she wanted to do. She stayed and she thought her life could pass like this, and was that such a terrible way to live?

He made no demands of her except to say he wanted her for life. *Do not say that to me.* And he said it again and she was silent, silent, then she pretended to sleep. She did not fool him though because he whispered it again in her ear. She ignored him. She tried out a vision: a future of them together—the regular trappings—the way she tried on a dress.

I want you with me forever.

Who knows about forever when I can barely see the day ahead?

Forever and I mean it.

You don't know that. How does one even plan for the rest of their life?

He sighed then and retreated to his side. He cloaked himself with silence as she had done so many times.

I need time.

He said nothing.

I don't know what I want.

Still he said nothing.

She left it and he fell asleep and she knew she lied to him and that she lied to herself. She knew what she wanted but her fear was greater and she was weighed with guilt and she hid behind a lie, a tired defence that had protected her so many times.

ADDITIONS

This would be her ninth. Lulu of the good figure, Lulu of the laugh, Lulu on whom they all had a crush. Amir once considered asking for her hand in marriage but reasoned she was out of his reach. Considering who Lulu ended up with, his chances were better than he'd thought them at the time.

For her first child, there had been excitement, congratulations, money in an envelope. For the second a gift, for the third something small. No one could remember what it was. For the fourth, the question: *Again?* And the fifth was much the same. Six, seven, eight—*they can't afford anymore*—and now the ninth, the wish there would be complications, that Lulu would need to abort.

In town, they smiled, they shook hands, the words were exact copies of the previous eight, but a curse had befallen them, like rabbits really, and in this day and age.

They discussed inviting her husband and giving him advice over cards: *Chemists, doctors, here is something you could use,* but none of them volunteered to look him in the eye and say the words. And—this was their conclusion every time—what business of theirs was it what Lulu and her husband did in their spare time, and what children were born as a result? He did not have to carry them on his head—and he said this to the rest— and they nodded. It was not their place but judging by their clothes and how rundown their house had become, a little money here and there was nothing major. And publicly weren't they the best of friends?

WARNING

It was their first proper fight. They both lost the battle. They both said, *Yes, this fight is a reference point in our lives.*

He had spent the evening with the boys and Jamila always encouraged him on this point. She knew it was the only time he saw his friends, it was the only free time in which they could talk.

Her first comment had been about Samir's wife. 'Doesn't she mind having you all around every night?'

'We sit outside. We are never in the house so we are not in her way.'

It was a comment—nothing—and he didn't give it another thought.

Later he saw that as the very start but Jamila insisted she never said the words he attributed to her, that if she said them they were innocent and she was making conversation.

A week later: 'Do the others ever bring their wives?'

Amir had been stupid enough to overlook the first comment. This time he looked up. This was not an idle question he could address with a word or two. There was more at stake than he had realised.

'Never. It is always just us. Some days, his wife has her friends over but they sit inside and I've never seen them.'

He wondered about bringing Jamila with him one time and he imagined how his friends would behave: polite, friendly, hospitable, but proper as if hosting the president. He imagined her trying to make conversation with Samir's wife, two women who knew how to talk and could therefore pass the time but without a point of commonality in their lives. It did not matter. It would not happen. He and Jamila would spend their days separate and alone, as long as each night ended in her bed.

He left it. No more needed to be said.

The following evening as she finished her tea, she told him she wanted to go with him to Samir's that night.

'Is it that you want to go out? Is it that you want to spend the evening together?'

'No, it's not that I want to go out but I want to visit Samir with you.'

'But why?'

'Because he's your friend.'

'But I have many other friends and we can visit them together if that is what you want but you know it's not proper unless you are my wife or we're thinking along those lines.'

'It doesn't have to be like that. Can't we visit people without being married? What is it with the people in this place, their stupidity, their fussiness, their gossiping all the time?'

He knew to be careful and he tried out many lines before stepping out cautiously as if to face a snake. 'We can go visit Samir, if you like, but it is not something I'd recommend.' He tried for lightness. 'Why don't you just marry me and we wouldn't be having this argument in the first place? Then we can visit all the people you want.'

She put her cup to one side. She wiped her mouth. She avoided his eyes. She let the silence grow. When he ventured her name, she shrugged and said never mind, and he was relieved by what he took for agreement that they would go to sleep now, that they could return to the peace they knew and liked.

When he woke in the middle of the night, he knew he was alone in bed. He found her on the roof smoking a cigarette. It was the height of winter and she was barely dressed. He kneeled before her and kissed her free hand, which was very cold.

'What is it that you want?' he asked.

'I just want a normal life.'

He laughed and remembered his marriage. All he had wanted was peace and quiet, all he had wanted was a simple love in their home.

A normal life. . . like the sort they lived here or the one she knew from her overseas life? Which one did she want and was it even in his power to provide?

He left it, he walked away, he thought about it for days after, he wondered about the impossibility of language, of being able to ever understand someone else. He saw the end much like a wave. It was rising over them and one day it would collapse on their heads but when he spoke like this, she laughed at him and said, 'It's not so bad.' But he foresaw it and he knew and it did not matter what she said. They could not live their lives here together without a union endorsed by the state.

It was foolish and her dreams belonged to another place and no matter their intentions and their hopes, these were dead fish that had no room in the life they shared in this place.

They were silent the entire way. He drove his car and their few attempts at conversation ended in silence. They had tried, he told himself later. They were both so desperate to keep the peace, to make it work.

Samir paused a second before he smiled and opened the door wide. 'Come in, come in, we're sitting in here,' he pointed to the living room, which Amir had set foot in twice before in his life. He and the others, they always went around the outside. That way, Samir's wife and children were undisturbed inside.

Jamila settled on the big couch and he noticed her eyes studying the contents of the room. She was discreet but he knew her and that this room was not to her taste, and he wondered if she was horrified.

Samir's wife came out and it was obvious she had thrown the robe on quickly and that underneath she was still in clothes for around the house.

The women talked and Samir called for a girl to bring tea and whatever biscuits they had in the house. He tried to remember the girl's name. Zeina or Zeinab or something like that. She was probably under ten and he thought the youngest was somewhere around five.

Samir asked about his day, a formal question they'd never used before in their lives. He answered—no swearing, his voice light—and he wanted a cigarette but Samir once said his wife didn't allow any smoking inside.

Later Samir will tell a story and he will wonder if it was from the time Jamila visited. *There is a camel so great yet it tries to tie its ankles so it is as slow as everyone else.*

He wonders about the camel hobbling about and how a camel in those conditions could ever be satisfied.

TAMING THE WOLF
(A FABLE)

Amir is hopeful.

It is another time, it is another life.

He thinks of the past, he thinks of the future, he thinks how nightly he tells Jamila, *You are the one I love.*

The past, he is sure, was a time he tried to carry a burden not his and pray emptily for life to flourish in a land that was hostile and also dead.

In the early days of his marriage, he loved his wife and badly wanted their union to work. He told himself things could be so much worse. He knew so many stories of men married to difficult women who counted the day they met as a curse. He did not feel like that. Not in the early days.

He remembers telling Samir his worries about his marriage.

Samir listened without replying, without making a single sound. Amir left that evening defeated, empty and alone, and knew it was more peaceful to leave her the bed and sleep on the couch.

Samir, his friend Samir, like a brother Samir, who did not make a sound. He felt foolish for speaking and he told himself from now on he would keep quiet about his burdens and he would not trouble anyone else with his woes.

That night, he slept terribly and many times he thought it should be morning but when he checked outside, it was still dark. He went through the following day as if in a haze and although he was tired, he went to Samir's just to get out of the house.

They had not yet started to play when Samir put down his cards and said, 'There is a story I wish to share with you boys.'

They put down their cards and waited. If only Samir could read and write, he could have shared his stories with the world.

'Once upon a time there was a lamb and there was a wolf, and both of them pretended they could get along.'

Amir avoided Samir's eyes but he listened and wished he had not come tonight so he could avoid hearing what Samir was about to say.

'The wolf had lived long among the sheep and could act like a sheep most days. And the lamb in our story thought the wolf knew enough about sheep that one day the wolf would grow wool and count itself as a lamb but we all know how useless such a hope is and that really such a thing would only happen when the sun rose from the west. Still, the lamb kept trying despite the wolf showing its teeth and threatening to eat the lamb alive. *These threats can't be real,* the lamb told itself. *There is no way the wolf will attack me as though I am any other lamb.* But one day the wolf did attack and I am not sure the lamb managed to escape with its life.'

Samir picked up his cards, lit another cigarette, and signalled they should continue with the round.

Amir did not speak his troubles to Samir again because his friend had heard and this would be his only reply.

Now he thinks about the story again and he wonders if once more he is trying to make the wolf into a lamb. The circumstances are different and if he were to compare Jamila to his wife, he'd struggle to find one way in which they are the same.

Still, perhaps the ground has no life and it is better to walk away. Or perhaps she does not respond to his proposals because she means soon to go away.

He can hope, as he then hoped, but if she leaves, she leaves, and if she stays, she stays and over the thing he desires the most, he knows he has little say.

HAPPINESS

They all called Rana a whore but none had the heart to say it to her face.

The facts: she was widowed at eighteen and had a child at nineteen. She never worked a day in her life and her child was often in trouble at school. *No aptitude* was written on the boy's report and they agreed the verdict was correct. She got engaged in her twenties but alas the relationship didn't work out and within two months they went their separate ways. She once spoke of her fears to a friend—*I worry that I will be lonely for the rest of my life*—but the friend was later found to have a loose tongue.

The friend admitted it herself that she had spread what Rana told her but as is often the case, she lightly changed what she had heard. *She is determined to find someone else. She doesn't want to be lonely. She needs a man in her life.*

These were the exact words of the friend. Someone who heard them made sure to write them down and then took the story back to the original source, saying, *This is what so and so has said.*

Those are the facts.

Here are the words that got around.

The child was not her husband's. He was born a month too late.

She needs to study, she needs to work. I wonder how she finds the money to feed herself.

It's not her family that supports her but a foreigner who is often out of town.

Even at school, she was already sleeping with the boys.

She should keep her nose clean and her knees together. What kind of mother is she to her son?

He heard these words. He could not avoid them. They were whispered behind his sister's back and the only true part was that her son was a royal brat. Twice he wanted to throw him off the roof and each time he had left without a word, shocked at how he could barely contain his rage.

More truths: he gave his sister money and so did his parents. His uncle abroad sent her money every month. The money arrived in envelopes but his uncle was a quiet man who said good deeds should be done in the dark, they should not be advertised with words.

He has two memories of her and they are there when his mind goes her way.

When Samir's sister was going to get married, Samir went personally to Rana's place and, over the fence, he invited her and the boy to attend. The night of the wedding, Rana looked again like a girl of sixteen. She danced the entire time, she clapped till her hands hurt and she later said it was the best night of her life. After everyone left, she made her way on foot through the dark streets of their town even though he said he could take her home. 'It is all right,' she said, smiling. 'I can see in the night-time and I am not afraid of what hides in the dark.'

She went away whistling, though she did not go to her own home but to their parents' place. She let herself in and the next morning, they found her sleeping in her old bed. She breakfasted with their parents and he was surprised to see her there when he dropped by. She rolled a cigarette for their father and one for herself and she said to no one in particular, 'Last night was the best evening of my life.'

That was the first memory and the second one was a happy one as well. In her forties, her son had gone off to his future and Rana met a man who worshipped her, who told her, *You shall be my wife*. They married without telling anyone and she packed up her home and moved into his house. Most days she smoked many cigarettes and her husband indulged her, which he later regretted when she spent the last decade of her life in ill health. Before she died, she wrote her uncle a letter to thank him for his years of support. She thanked her brother, her parents, she told her son to stay out of trouble. Finally, she made a phone call to Samir and said, 'I wanted to tell you directly how much that wedding of your sister's meant to me all those years ago. I know I don't have much time left and I can fairly say it was the happiest night of my life.'

She died—we all do—and while her misery would have been justified, he remembered her as always having a smile on her face.

THE LOVERS

FOR RODRIGO

An uncertain loneliness was his home. *You make a pact with the moon and the dream will come good.*
He wrote:

> *I want her, this companion, be she human or feathered and winged, be she a creature who lives in caves. I have done my penance. I am ready to shed my loneliness this final time, to make for her—this gift you send me—a place in my life.*

The moon was silent. He stared upwards in longing every night. He became a keeper of the moon, a tracer of this pale satellite. He wrote its patterns on pages that he fed to the fire at night because he may as well have etched the words onto his own heart.

The moon was silent for months. The moon did not smile. The moon never frowned. It is the serene face of eternity. None can make it tremble, none can touch its surface by reaching out.

He tried again:

You have become a symbol of my absent love. You are present in my life but you live beyond the reach of my hands. I mean for a possession, one of gentleness, kindness, and you have observed my life and you know these words are not lies.

The moon did not change in any way. The wave can smooth the rocks. The wind wears away at the cliff face so it does not hurt the world with its razor teeth, but the moon, his moon, their moon, was to be remote.

He took to praying and he was not a praying man. He flung his wishes into the face of the world silently, he wore a cloak of solitude, he forgot how he lived before his days were dictated by a futile hope.

One night, the lines began to arrive. They formed themselves like soldiers in his mind.

Isn't hope by its nature futile? It is the desire bared to the world, accompanied by the head that is bowed.

She will arrive. You are learned in patience. I make no promises about her timing or how long she will choose to stay.

You are not forgotten. Your wish is the wish of a billion others. It is the very beat of life.

He heard the words and he wrote them on a paper that he kept safe in his pillow as he spent his nights alone.

He was sleeping one evening, fitfully, his mind roaming through the years of his life, when there was a knock at his door.

Excuse me, is there anyone home? I am in need of some help.

He clothed himself and let her in to warm herself by the fire. He wondered about her. Perhaps she was a woman like all those other women who filled the world, with nothing to distinguish her from them, nothing that made her more his than anyone else's.

He wondered and watched her, careful not to let his gaze became a stare.

They had been together an hour when she shook herself like a creature that had emerged from the sea. 'I wish to tell you a story and I hope you believe what I have to say. A year ago I had a dream about this house of yours and the moon spoke your name to me. Those were the only clues I had: a vision of a home and then a name so I come here after a long search and I mean to ask your name. If it is the name the moon said, I will stay for all time and if not, then we will each go our own way.'

He hesitated. He thought about the moon. He thought about the words he had in his pillow, how he could quote them to her and hope that his visitor would remain. Instead he told her his name. She smiled and took his hand said, 'I think the moon means for me to stay.'

INERTIA

Jamila said she had come here for a month and she had now been here a year. She had needed a holiday, she said. She told people that even when they did not ask but one night, in bed, he asked what had really brought her here.

'I needed a break from my life.'

He nodded, lit a cigarette and she didn't say anymore.

When he left in the morning, she slowly got up and went to sit on the roof, a place she could visualise if she shut her eyes. There was the sea in front and the mountain at her back. She had settled into a routine, and while once the desire to escape had made her seek out this place, now inertia kept her here.

She had no wish to move, she didn't want to go to another place. Her days were repetitions, replicas of each other, and it shocked her to realise that this was what had driven her from the other place. Each day was a copy of the previous one and she went through her days in a fog. There were too many evenings when she came home to a dinner of tinned sardines before collapsing into bed, only to rise in the morning to repeat the pattern across the day ahead. She had fled not because she needed a holiday. Instead it was with the sense that *this is not a life*.

But she did not tell him this. She did not elaborate when she had the chance, and then as time passed it seemed unimportant to mention to him anyway.

Perhaps people make the decisions of their lives from a place of willpower but that has not been her experience so far. She goes some place, she does something without a reason in mind, and then she continues there because she cannot think of anything else she wants. It is a vine creeping through her life but she will not let anyone into the truth of her life. Let them see excitement. Who cares for the dull truth when a lie is shinier?

THE BED AND
THE TABLE

We all knew the story. Still we listen when Samir puts down his cards and lights a fresh cigarette and speaks of the disappeared, those we assume are likely dead.

To begin: we all knew her. Noura had lived in her apartment since we were kids. There had been a husband but he had died and her children were scattered, borne away by dreams and changes in the wind. (These are the words chosen by Samir who has this tendency towards poetry and words that rhyme and ring.)

Noura had fallen on hard times and her family propped her up because no one else would, but by her eightieth year she had outlived most of her relatives and whatever had been left to her by God's will.

We had seen her home emptied of valuables, her fingers stripped of gold over the years, until—as the story goes—she was left in that place with nothing but a table and a bed and her memories. It was enough, the rent hadn't been paid, the owner said, and four strong men were sent in to remove Noura and her possessions and dump them in the street, no matter her protests or the tears she shed.

We watched as the men carried Noura out with her lying on the table as if it were a bed. The table and Noura were placed outside the gate, and then the men went back for the bed and whatever else remained inside. All that time Noura cried and beat her chest.

When it was done, they locked the windows and the door, securing the place so she would have no way back in.

We helped her to her feet, we offered her something to eat. I want to tell you she found another home but the truth is that soon after, Noura disappeared.

The neighbourhood waited a week and when they heard she wasn't coming back, they broke the bed and table for wood, and who could blame them, because that winter was very cold indeed.

CHANCE

Jamila met Amir at a wedding. Really it was the stupidest thing. All those times she went with her family to a wedding and her mother pointed to a young man and said, 'What do you think of him?' And she considered the one that had caught her mother's eye to be the same as the others, also dressed in their best, dancing around him. She had hated how artificial it was, her prospective love singled out in this way as if they were out window-shopping. She wanted fate, destiny, the stars aligning.

So that wedding had been the universe's trick.

She passed him bread. He filled her glass. She considered his face nice enough and there was only one thing that distinguished that night from the hundreds of other weddings she'd been to. At the evening's end he said to her, 'I hope our paths cross again.'

The words were for her and no one else.

She weighed that sentence in her mind for a week, wondering why a sentence stayed with her when other words had completely disappeared.

She asked him later, 'Why did you say that to me?'

'Because it was what I meant,' he said seriously.

It was not the answer she craved, it was not the hand of destiny ordering her life. Instead it was a chance encounter that on another day would have failed to resonate.

Imagine her mother had pointed him out.

She shuddered.

It was the chance of it and her desire to weave it into a larger pattern that drove her to seek the fortune-teller she'd heard Samir speak about. 'She lives in the mountains. Anyone can tell you the way.'

She took her car and drove like a madwoman, wondering about the rationality of the details that make up a life. She found the fortune-teller, an ancient woman who babbled and had the appearance of being blind. *You speak to her and maybe she'll tell you something that speaks to your heart.*

She felt herself a fool for speaking to an incoherent woman who twitched and drooled, who smacked at her thighs to shoo away invisible flies.

The woman said nothing to her, nothing that stood out, except when she paraphrased the line of someone else. *We all find in the world what we seek.*

Jamila drove down the mountain with that line. She clung to it as if to a raft. She whispered it to him when she was sure he was asleep.

I sought you without knowing. I sought you as if in a dream. And now I wait to see what time will reveal.

He stirred and she kissed him. And then she returned again to her sleep.

VISITATIONS

Without telling anyone, his mother went to pay her a visit. Jamila was painting her nails on the roof, still in her bathrobe. She heard the knock and the maid answering the door, and she wondered which of her relatives it was this time.

It wasn't any of her relatives. It was his mum.

She debated meeting her in the living room, taking her sweet time doing her hair and make-up but it was defiance in the face of judgement that made her invite his mother to the roof where the sunshine might disarm her and allow Jamila the time to arrange her cards.

So this was his mother. In the photos Jamila had seen, she always wore a smile but now her face was serious as she politely accepted the chair that was pointed out.

This was his mother, this was the matriarch.

She realised how alone she was here. Her family had returned to the place they now called home, her friends were asleep on the other side of the world. She had no one to help her pick apart the significance of this visit, which broke with tradition and etiquette.

When he talked about marrying her, he insisted it must be done properly: his parents would call her parents, he would correctly ask for her hand. There would be no hiding, no mistaking his intentions, and she would be free of all doubt.

What then to make of his mother—alone—coming to visit her house?

They spoke as they had both been schooled to speak. The weather, the prices in the market, what the week held for each of them. She studied the orange trees below; she wondered what he'd make of this visit, if it would fill him with rage.

For a dove, use the usual traps but for a tiger, you'll need something else.

They went around and around, they joked, they laughed as if they were on stage reciting lines. After an hour, they walked out together and she waited at the gate until his mother drove off.

She went back inside and wondered how she'd break the news to him tonight.

When he came by, she suggested they go up to the roof.

It was close to sunset. They agreed it was quite a sight.

He put his cup down and she cleared her throat. 'Your mother came to visit today.'

He tensed but he held his tongue and clenched his fist. Then he shut his eyes, telling himself to relax.

'We had a good chat.'

'Did you now?'

'Yes. You could say that.' She lit a cigarette, offered him one, but he waved it away.

'What did she want?'

'She said I was welcome to visit anytime, that at a time convenient for us, she wishes to have us for dinner.'

'She said that?'

'That's what she said.'

'And what was your response?'

'I told her let's start with a cup of tea and see where it goes.'

He smiled then. Both possibilities were unconventional but it suited these unusual times.

Suddenly, he saw it had not been ruined, that his mother had not trampled the ground he had laid. Maybe, just maybe, his mother had added the fuel to finally make Jamila his wife.

KICKED IN THE PANTS

One day when she is alone, she will live her life.

It is a line that first occurred to her when she was fourteen and it is still with her at forty-three. She is going to live her life one day . . . in a distant future, her pieces will be arranged, she will know where she is going and then she will begin.

What she fears is legitimate. It is the breath at her neck that says, *You will never have your pieces arranged, you will never be alone. Listen, woman, your life is going to waste.*

She wakes sweating, she tosses, she turns and falls back to uncomfortable dreams.

In the morning, she tells him, afraid he will laugh.

Instead he takes her hand and kisses it and says to her, 'You had better begin because one day you will be dying and by then it will be too late.'

Now when she thinks, *One day, when I am alone, I will live my life*, she sees him before her, her hand raised to his mouth. She hears him saying, 'One day you will be dying,' and she rises as if kicked in the pants.

MONEY

When she hears of someone struggling, she wonders: how much?

When she hears they've fallen on hard times, she calculates quickly in her mind.

When it's *he lost his job, they've called their family for help*, she keeps an ear out in case there's no response.

He watches her at this and largely he keeps his thoughts to himself, except once he opens his mouth and says, 'You have to realise your money is not going to save the entire world.'

She is furious. She goes to say it's not like that, that's not what I thought at all, but he is right, so she fixes her hair and in the mirror practises her poker face so she can keep her thoughts to herself.

INERTIA II

One day she will be alone to do the things she wants. One day the stars will align, the sun will be just right, and then she can live her life as she wants. One day, someday, never day, a golden day, an olden day, she will be alone and there she is, living the life she wants.

Here she is, it is today, and she is alone at last.

Instead of freedom, she feels restless.

Instead of possibilities, she feels trapped.

The sea is before her, stretched beyond what she can see, and she cannot figure out if she should stand or sit, if she suffers from hunger or if she is in need of a drink.

She has dragged herself here, to drink at a fountain that has turned out to be a mirage. She contemplates returning home, packing up before an imaginary storm rolls in, but she doesn't.

She stays there, tied by her stubbornness as if an animal to a post, and thinks, I've driven myself here so I may as well enjoy the beach today.

Later when people ask about her achievements, how she rose so high, she looks at them baffled because it was dogged inertia all the way.

LUST

Amir was young, Jamila was young, their bodies not yet wearied with age.

He woke with her name in his mind and he was reminded of the emptiness at his side.

Her scent had long faded from the room and he did not want to be reminded of her with photographs and memories.

There would be no one to touch him, no one to offer the mercy of release.

He sighed and thought of her body again. In the glare of reality, he still had the comfort of her in dreams.

LESSONS

Her father is teaching her brothers. She is seven or eight, she is at her father's side, her hair done in pigtails, in a dress her mother has made for her. It is red and she still has it in a drawer somewhere. She likes the memory of the dress but it is gathering dust with the ghosts she has left behind.

To begin with: a lesson about choosing a wife.

'A woman is chosen for her beauty, her money or her faith.'

Her mother rolls her eyes. Jamila nudges her father. 'What about her mind?'

He smiles and tugs her hair. 'Also her brains.'

'Which is better?' asks Nazim or Ismail.

'Her faith, of course.'

Her mother puts down her cup of tea. 'You may as well continue the lesson. You have a daughter as well.' She fixes him with a stare that is a dare.

'Of course, of course, it is the same for a girl. She chooses a man for his strength or his money or his faith. Sometimes—in my case for example—he is chosen for his faith, but let us be honest, most women go for money because either they are stupid or they don't want to lift a finger.'

She looks up at her parents and tries to understand. 'Wouldn't it be best to choose someone for their brains?'

He puts her into his lap and hugs her. 'Yes, my dear, but to make a good choice takes brains and that is something most people today don't seem to have.'

LONGING

Every time she looks at the map at work, she picks out where he is and she imagines him walking in his part of the world.

He is so far away but his country is simply an area bordered by a line, and within that land he has a defined space.

She has no servants now. That was a luxury she could afford over there but here she does her own dishes, she opens her own gate.

She has mental conversations with him and each sentence begins with a word made of two sounds that represent him, that distinguish him in the emptiness of space.

Amir.

The word is a body that was once a smile but now it causes her pain.

The word is a man full of life and left behind, and she tells herself he belongs to the past.

The word is one she tries to erase from her mind but sometimes she thinks it and always with a sigh.

In her conversations with him, she explains herself, and he nods and tells her he understands. The reality is they agreed that they had no future, their paths converged briefly but it is better they each go their own way.

When she speaks to him, she asks who it was better for and that *more than anything, I wish to see you one more time.*

Only one more time. It is a point she emphasises, and she hopes the universe will grant her this because it has all the power in the world while she is only one being, her wish pitted against the others of the human race.

This is foolishness, she knows. It is time to move on with your life.

HOPE

Days and no word.

No calls, no messages.

It is the end, as they both said.

But there is hope.

One asks deep in the night: hope for what?

Hope for a return, hope for another chance, hope for the sound of his voice.

She waits, he waits. This impasse.

There is a message.

It is small.

It is nothing in the grand scheme of the world.

There is a smile.

Its name is hope.

CLICHÉ

If someone had predicted a future in which she lusted after a man from the village, Jamila would have laughed in their face. Such men were hard-headed, they thought to make a possession of their wife, and she was determined that she would never let herself fall for their sweet-talking ways.

She had friends who had fallen for such men. These men wove webs filled with castles in the skies. They promised the stars with tears in their eyes. They vowed to make the woman a queen, a singular imperial power over their male life.

And these women she knew—educated, intelligent, savvy, worldly women—fell for the lie. She put it down to their biological clocks. What else could explain how these women had lost their minds?

She saw the trajectory of such unions. A month after the honeymoon and already their faces were tired. Their plans were all routine and their choices mirrored those of their parents, only with a contemporary vibe.

She would not do that.

She would go and enjoy herself, she would allow no one to pry apart her thighs.

When she told him this, he laughed till he couldn't breathe, and when she told him to be serious, he lost the laugh but she could see the amusement in his eyes.

When she told him she wanted him forever, he said, Only if you'll be my wife.

When she told him she wanted to have forty children, all of them his (a biological impossibility), he said, We don't need to have children for us to live side by side.

When she told him her fears for the future, he told her to live with strength and to banish the demons from her mind.

When she told him she loved him, she imagined her friends laughing at her and saying, *Look who's fallen for the oldest cliché after resisting all this time.*

She argued with them afterwards in an imaginary debate. It was ridiculous to waste her time like this but it was her only defence against their attacks when she finally announced her little truth before the criticism of their eyes.

To hell with them, she whispered, and he asked her what was troubling her in the middle of the night.

Nothing, she lied, nothing. And it would be nothing, even if it meant staking her heart, mind and life.

THE STORY

This is the memory that is printed on her mind. Life starts in the concrete and then retreats to mental territory.

She resists attending the wedding. She has been resisting these social events. Secretly she thinks these people are backwards. Look at their ideas about politics and the country swamped with refugees. If only they stood on their own feet, the country wouldn't be a mess. If only they weren't so keen on handouts from overseas, this country would not be on its knees for fifty, sixty years.

She tires of the circularity of conversations such as these. She cannot stand the small-mindedness of the women and, yes, it is the lack of education, it is ignorance, but how does that help me when I try to converse with an imbecile who thinks the world is housework and dishes and that is all a person should aspire to in life? And the men who hide their weakness, who pretend they are in control of their little domains?

She is tired and she wants no more of it.

Still, it is her first invitation of this sort and so she attends, her lack of make-up an act of rebellion, her dress lighter, tighter than what the other women would recommend. *Let them talk*, she thinks. They will be done up like dolls while she has barely brushed her hair. Simpletons, and if they were before her, she would strangle them by the neck.

In the car, she lights a cigarette, the ash falling into her lap and making a mess, but she brushes it away and besides, the light will be dim and her lap will be tucked away underneath a tablecloth.

She greets, she kisses, she waves hello. *This is not my place*, but she claps on command, she smiles as a reflex.

When he sits down at her table with the others, he is distracted, his eyes are elsewhere. Her impression is of averageness; he is one of many and there is nothing to set him apart.

He smokes, he rolls up his sleeves, he eats absently, he asks her name, he asks how she's finding the place.

Distracted talk, round in a circle, she does not yet know she is trapped. He offers her a cigarette with his next one, lighting it for her before settling back in his chair. It is then she notices him and her mind goes to the future. She imagines their entire lives in an instant, she shakes her head as she shakes off the ash, and she refuses him as an option because he is not who she has in mind.

A man from her parents' village. That has already been done. And she sees her life then, how she has wanted greatness, how she has refused the common, and how much pain this resistance of hers has caused.

It is not a capitulation that she accepts him. He is nothing of the sort. If he was in a line-up of all the men in the world, he is still the person she would want. Even if she had her pick of other men—the handsome, the rich, the smartest, the fastest—he is the one she wants by her side and between her legs.

Whenever you are near, the world elsewhere ceases to exist. It is only you.

He laughs at this, her declaration of love, and he kisses her head, and later he will say: *Tell me again about the time we met.*

And she can predict his reactions, exactly the lines that will make him laugh, or those will make him so still it's as if he no longer breathes.

It always ends with a kiss: her mouth, her neck, the top of her head. He pulls her to him and he utters her favourite words. *There is no one else.*

FAIRYTALE

He said he loved her. The others said the same. He took her hand and kissed it and said, 'Wait here, I will only be gone a day.'

She waited, faithful like a dog. She kept herself entertained. She made up games about the clouds, she counted the white cars going past. She wondered did he mean a twenty-four-hour period when he said a day or another full day after the one when he'd left her? She should have clarified this and she resolved next time she would ask.

She waited and warmed herself with thoughts of him, she read the letters she carried in her bag, she smiled at this secret she kept that none could ever touch.

She waited and one sun set and then another, and she grew cold. She thought to seek shelter but she worried he would return and not find her and that would be the end.

She waited another day. She moved to a cover of trees from where she could see the spot he had last been seen. She dozed, she dreamed, she conjured up the sound of his voice.

On the fourth day, as she was telling herself that was that, he returned, shiny like crystal, and kissed her all over. *I am sorry, sweet thing, I am sorry I was kept away. I am sorry but it won't happen again.*

She kissed him and told herself the wait was justified. He was here and it was the same as it had ever been.

They spoke of the future and then he hid her in the cupboard. He called to her from the other side of the door, 'Just wait here where you will be safe. There is food and water on the shelf. Dangerous people walk by here so it is best not to call out.'

He left before she could ask if a day was twenty-four hours or another turn of the earth after the day he left. He made no promises this time but she warmed herself on the plans they made for the future. What was a little wait when eternity would be theirs? She waited and they laughed outside her door, she waited as she heard crashing and fighting, she waited as someone put their mouth to her door and whispered for her to come out. She sat still and told herself she was no longer in the world, anything to keep the dragons from eating at her mind.

She thought to read his letters but there was no light. She thought to eat a little more but she worried about her food running out. She thought to stand and stretch her legs but who knew what howled on the other side?

She thought about the passage of time, the universe contained in each minute that passed.

She thought about their future, she thought about when their future would finally begin.

She thought about when they met and wondered if it was the happiest day of her life or if it was the beginning of a curse.

She thought about this and their love and her devotion and her hopes and every single dream and how it was better for them to die than it was for her to lose her life. She said goodbye to him, silently in her mind, and she hoped he heard because she was taught to be kind, and with that she stepped outside. *One world has ended and I am afraid of what lies ahead.* Never mind. She walked out, thinking it better to face what was outside than die in the cupboard forgotten by the world.

ANGUISH

He is alone. Days alone, decades, centuries, each minute is the history of the universe. Alone, his private world. Once there was a skylight but the light has been turned off.

It is dark.

He often forgets to breathe. It would be easy to die if breathing weren't automatic. A reflex prompts him.

Inhale, exhale.

He forgets. He is weighed down by memories.

He thinks: I shall let go.

It is easier to stay alive than to find the strength to die.

Once upon a time there were lights above. Dark. It is dark.

He shuts his eyes. The darkness is resident in his mind. Inside, in his head, the worm in the apple.

Sometimes he sleeps. Other times he tries until he is too tired for wakefulness and then he slides bodily into the dreaming time.

POISON

She never meant to love across the lines.

She would love, of course, but religion was prerequisite number one. If he did not share it, he would not make the cut.

Her father explained it. A woman follows the man, not the other way around. She takes his name, his religion, she moves to the house he provides. She lets him drive the car, she lets him beat her for relief when he is down.

That is how it works so to ease the trouble, it is better to love and marry one of our own but even without love at the start, give it enough time and it will grow.

How long did she carry those words inside? Each time she loved a man, she wanted to parade her love, fling it in her father's face. It was a provocation, a declaration of war. It was revenge for the hurt of the words he had uttered in the past.

Her idea of love was demented. It was a misshapen creature. Give it wings of bamboo but no matter the love and attention and devotion you lavish on it, you cannot make this creature fly.

How many broken birds did she nurse in the dark? Each of the men said, *Thank you, see you later, I had a nice time*, and she was left with her rage and the poison of her father's words as she wondered if he was right.

She had tried the wrong places.

She could not make a dead bird fly.

Jamila, give up, no love is written for you at this particular time.

She should twiddle her thumbs, she should plant some trees. That is how she could find peace once more in her life.

She waited . . . a spider in the dark, biding her time. She waited so long she gave up and forgot what she was waiting for. It was something—a sense perhaps—but her memory was faraway, and she loosened her hold on it until it floated away into the unknown, and with this freedom, she found she could once more live her life.

TWO

LOVE

From early on, I sensed your solitude. You were like an
island alone. What interested me was that you were yourself and you would only permit people ever so close.
I remember this now because I read my notebooks recently.
Lately I want to keep you to me. It is something I tell
you repeatedly. I sense you carry a lot of sadness inside
and I would like to hunt these dark animals you keep and
rid you of them but I do not have that power. Even if I
knew every little detail about you, even if we spoke
endlessly for the rest of time, I would still not have this
power, not even if I knew you from the beginning of our

lives. There are limits to how much a person can occupy another person's life. There are limits. We are humans. Our days are not endless. Our days are finite. We will die at our appointed time, and when that day comes, I do not want to die wishing I had told you I loved you, wishing I had bared my heart to you when I had the chance. I do not want to die with regrets. I wish to live freely and with courage and to give you all of my love.

I could write more words. I could defend, expand and explain but words such as these need no extra support. They can stand on their own, as we stand in each other's lives, as a presence, as a witness, as a person who loves the other unconditionally, as a person who walks towards someone even when they are afraid.

So many things grow quietly in the silence. They are there with us at this distance when we are apart. There is the silence. Let our love always be great.

You do not need to put on a show for me. I don't need to be entertained like a child. The tricks and charms you wear for others have no home in the place I occupy with you. Each day I shall love you without the antics we perform in the hope of being liked. Put them to one side when you come to me because it is the truth I came for, not the pleasant fantasy of a shining lie.

From the day I met you, I sensed your openness to me. I sensed that you were available, that whatever space you inhabit is a space you would share with me. I arrive here to share it with you, be it lavish like palaces, be it the bareness of your body that nightly occupies my dreams. Your presence is a phantom when you are not around. Your voice is a phantom limb. Some days I string together sentences and it is as if you speak them with your phrases and I receive them on the inside of my ear.

These words I write have a meaning and it is love, though we are separated by the greatest ocean in the world. It is possible for an ocean to separate bodies but not two spirits connected before time even began. You are like eternity to me and I exhaust myself with what I wish to say to you.

I want to draw you close so you are against my heart.

I want to give you so much pleasure because to me, you are passion and desire, and they are intertwined.

I want to imprint myself upon your life till you know you will never again walk alone.

I am here for you, I am here, I am here for whatever time fate has given us in this life.

I am here before you and I say this to you as always with all my love.

THE VEGETARIAN

Jamila woke Amir at three in the morning to tell him about the time she tried to save the world.

Later he thought about her words as he dressed for work. Later he wondered if he had hallucinated their conversation, if Jamila telling him a story while he was half-asleep could be called a conversation.

It started when she was fifteen. She wanted to save the pandas and tigers, she wanted to chain herself to a tree. The older the tree, the better.

I told my parents we had to cut meat from our diet.

I told my family people like them were ruining the world.

So I became a vegetarian. I wanted to shave my head but my dad would have locked me in my room until my hair grew back.

Amir imagines her in a room alone, waiting for her hair to grow back so she can go outside. He imagines the walls are bare, the room illuminated by a small window covered with bars. He imagines her refusing food in the middle of a hunger strike.

When he describes his vision to her, Jamila laughs so hard she begins to cry.

Chances are I had enough books and magazines and CDs to keep myself entertained for months. I wouldn't have lasted an hour on hunger strike. I just don't have the capacity for grand political gestures.

He is puzzled and he asks how long her vegetarianism lasted.

'It was less than a month.'

Amir suspects it was closer to a week but he says nothing because he doesn't want to force her into a lie.

At times, he imagines her as the vegetarian on a hunger strike, and the thought of her without any hair still makes him smile. His smiles lasts a second and then he remembers this is his vision and the reality was not what he has in mind.

They are out on the street and she speaks of the people they know.

It is so nice Khadija has the support of her family, that she can live with her children under her parents' roof.

He does not tell her that Khadija has no means of supporting herself, that her ex-husband is a coward, and that Khadija lives with her children in her parents' house because she has no other choice.

I like that people here have not lost the simple joy of living. They eat in a simple way, they gather together for all their meals.

It does not matter that there is bickering, that people get on each other's nerves, that patience and tolerance with one's family are already stretched so thin.

I like that couples get married and that then they are together for life.

That's because they cannot afford a divorce. It would put too much pressure on their families to separate, so they are resigned to their disagreements and nightly they argue behind closed doors.

I like that . . .

He interrupts her before she can say another word. *Remember you told me you became a vegetarian? And how afterwards you went back to how you ate before? You had a choice, a luxury that people here do not have. I could not be a vegetarian, no matter how much I wanted to because I would not be able to survive. People here stay together because they have no other choice. Khadija lives with her parents because her other option is the streets. If you told her right now,* You can have a place of your own but it's on the other side of the world, *she would leave with her children immediately, even if it meant never seeing her parents again.*

She avoids his eyes. *You misunderstand me. I do not mean to romanticise their lives.*

The truth hurts her so he keeps quiet.

THE LOVERS

They continue on, talking and walking aimlessly.

There is the love between them, obvious to the casual eye, but some days he wonders about this separation in their lives.

LAMENT

There is the silence that can be filled and there is the silence that cannot.

I think these words with the knowledge I will never say them to you.

I think of our future and I fear that what we have is all there is.

I know that the world prizes the man for his money and I reject this but will we be comfortable on what you earn, will your pride suffer if we spend instead what I have?

I have these ideals and I have carried them all my life, ideals of how I wish to live in defiance of society, and I am afraid that despite my ideals and hopes, time will prove me weak.

I wonder if we should have children, if this isn't one more trap for a woman's ankle to a man's until the inevitable resentment kicks in?

Will we resent each other in time? Will we become first comfortable and then indifferent and then will our hearts become hard and cold?

I pose these unanswerable questions but I do not ask them of you because I do not think they are fair. I do not wish to burden you with the thoughts that cross my mind.

Would I be content with the normal life we'd have together?

Would I be content for us to have coffee in the morning, to kiss you goodbye, and then go about our separate days like couples all over the world?

I want to be content with this.

I want to say it will be enough but I fear my restlessness, that I lack the staying power others have.

I refuse to say this to you because I love you and I tell you this every day. I could not bear your disappointment or, worse, could not bear to discover that you predicted this and in fact you understand.

I don't know, I don't know, I don't know a thousand times.

I write this while sitting across from you and I ask you what it is that makes you smile.

You tell me it's this—us together—the companionship after each of us being alone.

My thoughts are a betrayal. I wish to be cured of them because they make me so afraid.

TOGETHER WE WERE ONCE UPON A TIME

I wish I had known you when you were young.

I wish I had known you when you were five.

I imagine you like this, the child version I have seen in photos. I see you with a backpack on your way to school.

I think of us together in the same class. Perhaps it would not have worked as I imagine in this alternative life. We might have been in different classes or else our schools might not have been the same.

I imagine watching you across a desk, our love beginning so young. We could have been two trees, our lives growing in parallel.

I think of you older. You are ten, twenty, then you are thirty-five. Then we are old together, we have known each other all our lives.

There is a sense when you meet someone. You talk, you discover each other's lives. I have had this sense with you. We have known each other once, we were separated and then we came together later in our lives.

I do not see the time before I met you as a waste. I know that no matter how much time we have together, it will never be enough.

It is an endless well. You are at the end of the tunnel and I am forever swimming to your side.

DESPAIR

The end
we carry it with us
from our start

In the end, she felt despair.

There is a photo of her in her parents' house. She is aged six. She has a crooked smile for the camera. The world is a paradise still.

Long ago, there was a summer on the beach. There were the countless consecutive days when they would go early and not leave till it was dark. There were the days of blindness, when one avoided being beneath the sky because the sunlight was too bright. As the summer dwindled, she despaired at the end of the holidays, that soon she would be back at school and it was not enough to have the compensation of her friends.

Her father used to laugh at her tears when they left the beach, at how she cried over the last swim, the last ice cream, the last barbecue in the park nearby. *It is the last one now*, he told her, *but summer always comes again.*

It is not enough. It will never be enough to stare in wonder at the stars unreachable and far away. It is not enough to love and have it die despite your hopes and have someone tell you, *It is all right. Love will come again.*

What if it does not, she whispers to herself, *what if summer only exists as a promise and I never see the sunshine again?*

You're being melodramatic, her father said to her whenever she was tearful. But you grow to adulthood and no one thinks you need comforting again. There is the assumption you will manage by squaring your shoulders and arranging your face before the world.

In the end, there is no comfort. There is no word that will give her peace at all.

It is over. It is time to walk. There is a wall and its name was always despair.

THE LETTERS

1

The things I wish to say to you, the things I wish to do, they multiply. When I shut my eyes, day and night, there you are. Your face I have memorised but I wonder if I will see you in this life again.

Why did we walk from each other? What impelled us to walk away from a love like ours? What craziness, what lunatic possession convinced us that it was better to leave than to turn around and fight? You know that movie I love—the one where the hero is chased until he is cornered in a tunnel and only then does he turn and fight. I feel like that now, that I no longer wish to be away from you, no longer do I accept the premise that we must be apart. No, my love, it is time to hold one's ground, it is time for us to reverse our course and prepare to fight.

What is the alternative? You are all things intelligent and I know that the future weighs ever on your mind. What is the alternative? We both leave, we both continue to walk away, our love becomes disused and empty like the broken cities of the world, and in time our great love will lie down for the final time and at last it will die.

And what happens then? There will be regrets, there will be bitterness, there will be the conclusion that life is unfair, that the world has nothing to offer us—we who wished for passion and a colourful love. The world offers us nothing. We will surrender our other dreams as we did the greatest thing in our lives. What is it to hand over the little that remains when the greatest has already been lost?

I write this, I send it, and it is with a spirit of hope. Countless times we marvelled that despite our differences we two are cut from the same cloth, were born of the same spirit, that never have two people been so united in the outward expression of their lives.

Do you remember we said that? Do you remember we both agreed?

So I write this with the hope you still agree, that we can build a future together, one of harmony and kindness and our love, which has been the best thing in all the days of my life.

I remember always the day I met you. I remember it as a day of music and sunshine and curiosity. I remember you always as a spirit of light.

What do you say? What about we give this another try? Can we return to the day we parted and from there we pick up the thread and see if we can't be companions who care for each other till the end of time?

2

Do you remember how our days used to begin? Do you remember that one would wake the other with a kiss? What lightness to begin the day like this! I feel an absence from how those days used to begin. If there is one thing I miss above all others, it is that kiss.

We are separated and it is no one's fault but our own. Yes, there is an ocean between us now but we chose to put an ocean in our path. We chose this as we once chose to begin the day with a kiss.

When I remember those days, they seem to me to be days of sunshine, days of leisure that collected together too quickly to become a year. I remember keeping track of those days with you: *It's been a week . . . a month . . . three months . . . do you realise we have been together an entire year?*

We never meant for it to be a year. We fumbled like children. I can write this here: that we were like children in our love. There was an innocence and we thought, as all lovers must think, that nothing could interrupt the spell in which we lived. But it was interrupted, and the world is faultless, and instead we are the guilty pair.

I do not want these to be letters of blame. I do not want to fixate on a specific moment when our course was changed. Perhaps you will agree on the moment, perhaps you will not, but that is not the purpose of these letters anyhow.

I shall tell you what I do know, what is a conviction in my entire being.

I loved you and you loved me, and there is no reason that we had to part. We can come up with stories about why we are not together, stories that will convince another person's ears, but there are no reasons, no version that I accept peacefully. There are none and I don't believe there ever will be a set of facts that will persuade me of the soundness of the mutual decision we made.

We were very solemn, we were like businesspeople. We could have shaken hands, and this is where we went wrong. There was a morning that did not begin with a kiss. It was this empty morning that undid the future in which we had begun to implicitly believe. If I were to blame something, I would blame that morning or else it would be our foolishness. We were so innocent in our belief, in our trust, in our openness, in how we took to each other as if alone we could no longer breathe.

Come back to me. Do not hide from me. Do not keep from me to honour a decision we made together, even though it dishonoured us both. Do not hide away because of a sense of pride. Do not keep away because you believe I have lost interest. I have not. If for whatever reason I should find you changed or that your love for me is not what it once was, I would count it the tragedy of my life.

Come back to me. You will find no aspect of my love has changed. The person you met at the beginning is the same person who takes the time to call you back, so that once again our love has every chance to flourish in our lives.

3

Do you remember the first time we fought, how we were shy afterwards like lovers before their first night? I remember being afraid. What if this was the end and you decided to send me away? My terror of abandonment was at the forefront of my mind. And then there was the weariness. How exactly do we recover the ease that existed between us only yesterday?

I made you coffee and presented it to you in the hope you would notice me and smile. A smile would mean that there was a way back from the argument of the night.

You were sad. It was plain on your face. And it occurred to me that I would prefer to hurt myself a thousand times rather than see that sadness again on your face. Even after we spoke of it, your sadness lingered, I think, for days. I am tired, you told me, and I believed you but I should have realised it was your sadness still and it hung over our heads. A similar sadness hangs over my life now that you have left.

When I think of the future, when I think of seeing you again, I wonder if we can return to how we were before, if we can meet each other again with the ease and openness that we both expected when we were face to face. I know things have changed, I know they will not be the same, but I think of seeing you relaxed again, your presence like a smile, a symbol that joy will find its place between us again.

4

Do you remember our former separations? You once said you could only bear a few days. Here we are and now it has been weeks.

The first time it was a day, one whole twenty-four-hour period, and when I saw you at the end of it, I thought, *I hope we never have to do that again.* I told myself, *Come on, you're being silly, these theatrics over being apart a day.* For most people, this is routine, for most people, this is commonplace but why should I judge my love with you by what others are accustomed to? Let them be parted for a day and not blink at the absence. Let them calmly go about their day of emptiness without an ache. Let them be sensible adults while I call on heaven and say, *God, please do not subject to me this again.*

You are the one who told me to drop this urge to compare, to quantify the mystery of intangible things. *Why do you do this when there is no answer, no comparison? Why do you subject the contents of your heart to a running race?* Yes, they are content, they are unaffected if their beloved is distant for a day, but I am not and I refuse to be, and I do not want your absence to be commonplace and expected, something that I should take in my stride. Worse, imagine I begin to welcome it. I mean this in all seriousness but I would prefer to take a gun to myself before I accept your absence as ordinary as putting on my clothes.

5

We are separated by an ocean now as we were separated by it before we met. The difference is our consciousness. I did not know of your existence, your life on the other side of the world. I was not conscious of being cut off from the world. The ocean I knew every day of my life was the horizon. It was the backdrop of my life but now it takes on the character of a barrier. It is the wall between me and the one I love. Once it was an ocean I swam in, its waves known to me as far back as the stretches of my memory. I never saw the ocean before but now it is all I see. I have this vision that if I take a boat out onto the water and row beyond the horizon, I will find you there waiting for me, a creature born of the sea. I will touch you with my hands and mouth, and I will remember that before I met you, before I tried to claim you, you had your life at the end of the ocean, that you are your own world, that before I attempted the futility of possession, you had constructed a tower of yourself and placed it at the world's edge.

How do I call you back, the one who has slipped from my life? You are a figment of my dreams and if it weren't for the few photos I have, I would doubt your existence completely.

Except you are real. You exist. You do not belong solely in the world of memory and dream.

I imagine us again. I imagine a scene like one from a film. We run to each other, you are once again in my arms but I know you, I know myself, and chances are we would be struck shy all over again.

I am not one for faith, I am not one for God, but I find myself bargaining with the One in the middle of the night. *Grant me this, only this, and I promise, I the faithless believer, that I will never ask you for anything again.*

6

I imagine you as a child. I imagine you before the world and its sadness has touched you. I imagine you before you learned of heartbreak and the lessons it teaches. I am not here to glorify pain, not when I wish for your love in my life.

We assume in surveying our lives that when it is asked of us, we will be able to love with the purity of poetry, that we can bare ourselves, when in truth we cannot imagine our existence without the protection of clothes.

I imagine you as a child because it is the part of life still resplendent with possibilities. Life is difficult; it bites at the spirit and it trims the edges of our hope. So I imagine you as a child, full of smiles, your hair lighter before it was darkened by time. I imagine you as this child that you assure me is nothing like the child you were. *I was despondent, I raged against the world.* From a distance, the image is one that makes me smile but close up, I want to soothe your fears and rage.

With you, I recovered the innocence of childhood. I remembered a time when I believed I could love completely. It was you who returned that paradise to me.

7

Do you remember the nights I loved you?

Do you remember you were mine in the night-time hours between dusk and dawn?

Each day for me your body was a continent that I wished to explore with my hands and tongue. I wanted to burn myself upon your skin so that later you would remember and the memories would make you blush.

I wanted knowledge of all the tricks that would please you and I wanted to do them again and again.

I miss your body. I will not lie. I miss that our times in bed were an expression of our love.

When I think of you leaving, I believe I could die. I say that it was our decision to break apart but the truth is you are there and I am still here. One of us has left and the other is too immobilised to do anything but stay.

I write you these letters and I sense I could throw them down a well for all the good they will do. I will not send them because I have my pride and I do not wish to beg.

What saddens me the most is that for all our talk of love and how we would honour it, we fell into the same traps as everyone else, and no matter how great our love, in the end, like those sad stories, it could also die.

LINES FLOAT IN AN OCEAN IN A LETTER OF LOVE

The tenderness of strangers on the street.

A father pulls his child close and hugs him till the child protests. *My bones begin to hurt.*

Your ankle tied to mine in a dream.

When I cried, there were tears in your eyes. When I laughed, you said I was so alive.

The possibilities of life unfold fruitful when we are side by side.

The smell of you after you have taken me inside.

Every story, every poem, every film ever written about love, no matter how clichéd.

Your hand on my arm as if that is where it belongs.

I cannot lose you. I cannot bear the emptiness of a colourless life.

An old couple pressed together, each thinking: *The other is my life.*

The recognition that Gibran was right. Stand together yet not too close. You are but the witness to the other's life.

There is a memory of you. It is summer. You breakfast in shorts and a shirt. You are the centre. The universe is a stage for my beloved to live out a golden life.

I wish you sunshine and warmth for every day of your life.

Dance, my love. The world is glad you are alive.

8

Do you think the weariness of routine settled in? We had no fights, we had no arguments, it was not even the rot of complacency. Perhaps we knew what to expect here, our passion cooled, and then we each wished for colour elsewhere in our lives. I offer this by way of explanation for why we walked away. There are many factors and I am hitting blindly in the dark, but did we decide love itself was not enough? It reminds me of that film you like where the girl says towards the end: *Can one ever have enough of love?* Can this question ever be asked? Is it a legitimate question at all? At what point does one have enough of love, at what point does one abandon the boat for a future that cannot yet be seen? Did we underestimate what it takes to tend love, to protect it so that it can warm us in the darkness and the light? There was a point when you grew distant and I knew it but would not admit that your mind and heart had already left. You were still present, you made the usual jokes that we both liked but they were words said to fill the time and they lacked the life they once had.

Perhaps I expected too much, placing too great a weight on our love beyond what it could bear. Perhaps my mistake was to make you the centre of my life when to you this was temporary and your future lay elsewhere. It is a question I offer with the awareness that it has no answer, that I will not send these letters I write you, that their end is the grave silence of eternity.

ENDINGS

She imagines it and how it will be.

As he once slipped into her bed, she slips into his city easily.

There may be a spot of awkwardness. It is a cloud that will pass.

They will be reunited. They will laugh. Perhaps they will cry as well.

They will agree: let us never be parted ever again.

LEAVING

She is leaving, she is leaving. She has already left and he watches her exit the room.

He means to call out.

He does nothing.

He does nothing at all.

She leaves and he is left behind.

It is not what he imagined as their end.

It is not meant to end like this.

THE PIANO

There is a park with a bench around the corner from her house. Sometimes she goes there in the middle of the day and it takes her a long time to realise it is because someone plays the piano in an apartment overhead. She had thought her choice of place and time was random.

The music she hears triggers a memory. She is with him again and they are ready to dine. In the restaurant, a piano is played out of sight. She comments on this and he looks around and says, 'How do you know it is live?'

She pauses and considers the question, struggling for evidence to support the sense she has. In the end she can only shrug. And she thinks, *If you knew a thing or two about music, you would know this is live.* Except she does not think this but says it aloud, and she is embarrassed by her blunder which has the power to harm him in the world outside.

He lights a cigarette and says with a directness she does not like, 'Am I not refined enough to tell if a piano is being played live? Am I better suited to card games because that is the destiny of someone in my station of life?'

She hates this directness. It makes her want to hide. She knows she should apologise but if she does, it will give greater weight to the mistake she's made, and it will be lodged forever in his mind.

She considers her options. She can apologise or attack. Is it possible that their entire relationship can be undone by the slip of a tongue?

But was it merely a slip? Is there more at stake than repeated professions of love in the night?

She apologises. Of course she does, and he accepts it as one does the apology of a silly child. It has passed . . . yet it does not, and later, he kisses her goodnight, and he promises her he is not angry, they will speak in the morning. *Forget it, you have apologised enough.*

She realises now he lied to her and she believed him, and once this piano made her miss him but these days it makes her cry.

THE MAGPIE

At the time of his death, Amir took on a magpie's form.

This was a dream she'd had before. He dies and she is in widow's clothes and it does not matter those who tell her that white is the colour of death, that the soul is pure, it is now with God.

Black is my mood, black is the ground in which he has been enclosed, black is the world where once upon a time there was light.

In the dream, he is a magpie and she is another bird. They wheel and dive, they talk in different tongues but one another they understand. It troubles her that she cannot see herself, that she can see him clearly but is unsure of her own form.

When she wakes, she is in tears, and she realises her emptiness is because the truth is reversed. He has disappeared. She cannot see him anywhere, not even if she shuts her eyes. She has her human form and she needs photographs to remind her of his face so she can fill in the fantasies she has of him at night.

She speaks to him but never is there a response.

She is alone in her bed, she is alone at home once more.

The only time she is not alone is when she sees one of his birds. This is a bird that speaks, its deathly blackness and the patches of white. It rolls sounds into a song and she imagines him speaking to her from the lamppost.

Her friends tell her to go out. They tell her to not spend so much time alone.

She considers catching an army of magpies and freeing them within the walls of her home. They can fly in circles, they can beat against the window as they seek to free themselves from her trap.

She could capture it. The magpie she sees today is the same one each time and it has become friendly in recent days.

She imagines holding this bird, stroking its black-and-whiteness, and with a kiss bringing it into the house where it belongs.

The world will not miss this bird. Its mate will not call out its name. Its children will grow into their lives and her loneliness will not hurt so much.

She could have trapped him. She could have begged him to stay. She could have used the tricks women use but then he would have been her magpie in a cage.

She leaves it, this uselessness, this empty dream. She says goodbye to the bird—her companion—and slowly returns to the world.

THE DOG IN THE ROSES

This was Samir's favourite story and any one of us had heard it many times. Had Samir been interrupted, any one of us could have recited it word for word, line by line.

One time there was a dog who lived at the bottom of his world. I am being polite of course because I know, as the dog knows, that what he calls a home is actually a slum, and rather than call it a slum he calls it a home in the hope of making you think it better than it is. I don't want to hurt the dog so I will say this quietly behind his back and hope he never hears. His slum of a home had garbage everywhere, human waste was what the dog walked through, and while one can dress it up with positivity and hope, let me tell you that there is a big difference between the smell of a rose and the smell of shit. So while the dog liked to believe in roses and he saw them in his dreams, his actual days were less than ideal.

So one day, for some reason or other, the dog saw a garden of roses and it became his most pleasant memory. The roses were better than the pictures, the roses were better than the ones he had seen in films, but a day is not a life and the dog found himself again in his slum of human shit.

Once he had imagined it was better than it was but now he could not ignore what he smelled and what he walked in and how he literally lived in a human tip. Once he had seen the sky and he had seen the clouds, and he had done his dog-best to have optimism and hope and to believe in whatever other lies we tell ourselves when it's ourselves we wish to deceive.

He tried to keep his spirits up, he tried to keep his smile, but he knew about the roses now, how they were better than the pictures, better than those famous films, and he decided then that unless he had the roses, he might as well not live.

THE CHILD OF THE SEA

Jamila's belly is large and he thinks, *How could she have hidden her state from me?* Overnight her stomach holds a child and he does not understand how he did not notice sooner. Only last night he had run his hands over her stomach but now he sees her cross the street and there is that funny walk pregnant women have.

Why has she hidden it?

Why didn't she tell him?

It confuses him. He should have known.

She is on the promenade. She talks to a stranger, a habit of hers. He once chided her for this friendliness and she shrugged and said they were different in this respect. *Why must I go through my life aloof from the world?*

She was right but it was not a habit he could fall into any more than she could stop this friendliness of hers. Perhaps it is women and their chattiness and how they see the world. It is an extension of their softness, their bodies, the sweetness that is theirs alone.

He shakes his head. Her state has gone to his head and made his brain soft.

He has heard her tear to pieces someone who has slighted her.

He has heard her argue down men twice her size and refuse to give ground, even when they moved in to intimidate her.

She calls him the sentimental one.

He stares at her.

She is carrying their child. This is the child they were meant to have.

When will their child be born?

He wants to call to her.

Jamila, what shall we name our child?

Jamila, are we going to have a child?

Jamila, you are my love.

Jamila, Jamila . . .

He shakes himself. She has disappeared in the crowd.

On the day their child is born, she kisses Amir and hands him their child.

At some point, our child will need to feed.

Jamila's hair is loose and she wears a dress. She is barefoot and he wishes to tell her to protect her feet, that there may be glass that will cut her as she walks near the sea.

He is trapped with a breathing child. Already their child is two or three years.

She walks out of their house into the glare of the sun, her hair like seaweed, her dress clinging to her body, the one he wishes to possess nightly and which now belongs in the land of dreams.

Jamila, his walker, Jamila, who is free. He calls to her but she is beyond him. She dives into the water. She is there but then she is not, and their child, the one he holds, the one that breathes, calls to her and then dissolves like a wave back into the body of the sea.

THE BIRD

Your bird died today. Your spirit left the room.

I wonder about this omen.

We lived our lives separated and destiny allowed us a return, a turn together, which is denied to others in this world.

I content myself with imagining a reunion. I imagine if there is nothing, there is only darkness at our end, that I shall never see your face again.

How does one make a life bearable if one is denied the hope of lightness, of something better than this valley I find myself in?

YUMNA KASSAB

People are filled with advice. They mean well, I know, but I wish for this solitude so I can be alone with you.

I will not condemn myself to this loneliness forever. What a waste to squander our happiest moments together!

I am alone. In a few minutes, I may change my mind. I am alone and I have not been alone in so long.

The bird has died. I buried it as I never expected to bury you. Your body is in the ground but your spirit, it leaves, but then again I feel it here.

My mother comforts me with a story. The spirits who are together at their end. It is only a story—symbolic of course—but I feel protected by it. The universe has its promise, it is full of possibilities. Who am I to say what awaits us on the other side?

If there is nothing, I will at least know that with you I was alive.

If there is something, like the story of the lovers, I hope we find each other, my lovebird, once again.

DREAMS

It was a dream. Jamila knew this because she was in a place she had never been before with Amir.

He was walking from her. She called to him but the wind took away her words and he continued to walk as if he had not heard her.

You are my love.

You are everything.

Please don't walk away from me.

But Amir walked and he walked into the wind and he disappeared, and when she tried to think of his name, it was as if he had never existed, as if she had never known him.

He woke in tears. He had been dreaming. Jamila was trying to touch him but her hands passed through his body as if he belonged to air and did not exist.

He could hear her. She was calling but he could not make out her words.

He used to think that he would never erase his wife's craziness but Jamila banished all thoughts of the past. With her, he achieved a state that he believed was pure fantasy. The rest of the world disappeared, it ceased to be, and yet in these dreams, he was the one fading, he saw again her hands pass through him, her mouth spoke but nothing could reach him, not her words, not her hands, he forgot all memory of her kiss.

He would have taken this dream to Samir for interpretation but already he knew what Samir would say. *You had a love and you let her get away and now she fades from your life for good.* Samir needed no cards, no sand, no coffee to make sense of these dreams. Their meaning was obvious but this did not reduce the loneliness Amir felt.

He thought about calling her. It would be late morning her time. He thought about it, dismissed the idea, ordered himself back to sleep.

He may have cried but finally sleep—elusive—came for him.

DROWNING

She never tells Amir about the dream. How can she? No matter how she explains it, no matter how much she reminds him the dream is not real, it is a betrayal. The worm is in her subconscious, and when she is not paying attention, it will make a break for the surface, and she will betray both him and their love.

In the dream, he is drowning. He is in the surf, the waves are rough and she is at a distance watching on.

He is a human being dying. He could be any human, in fact, and she feels no connection to him. She is not tied to him.

If he dies, it is okay, she will move on.

The mind has forgetfulness and ultimately this will protect her from memories of him.

In her mind, she urges him not to cry out, not to call her name, to go ahead and die, relinquishing any hold he has over her.

She watches his struggle. He is any human, he is any beast. We are born, we live and then we die at our time.

This is his time, she says, and like that she is released from anything that binds her to him.

She turns and walks away. She is thankful the waves are loud, that they hide his cries.

She asks the world to wipe him from her memory. This is freedom . . . to be oblivious to someone else's cries.

She walks away and she does not once glance back.

She assumes he drowns and the thought is enough to end the dream. It forces her to wake once again in tears.

TOUGH LOVE

He has lost once before, he has now lost again. The days pass painfully and he's had enough so he goes to Samir.

His friend is seated around the back of the house on the floor. The fire is lit and the wind shakes the weak walls.

He speaks and speaks until he's empty of words and then Samir holds up his hand.

'You say you love her but you let her leave when you should have tied your leg to hers. You come here speaking of love and it is an insult to me and my wife who is the mother to my kids. It is an insult to the love I have for my parents who are thirty years dead. You talk of love but

237

either you're a liar or you're weak, which, in either case, amounts to the same thing. The universe gives you the greatest thing it has and you spit in its face by rejecting it. The two of you agreed to shake hands and go your separate ways. If Rayan said tomorrow she was going to the moon, I would be on the first plane. If I said to her I was going to Mars, I am certain she'd say, *Give me a moment while I prepare the kids and their things.* If love comes into your life, you hold on to it. That is what you do. I can lie to you and say sweet words but they would be an insult to our friendship, to your intelligence and pride. It is easy for your tears to fall on my knee, for you to cry like this before a friend but you cannot pick up your phone to give her a call. I don't have time for lies, I don't have time for games so don't bring your pain to me again. Either you are a man who does what needs to be done or else you come here and we pretend she does not exist. Here is a cigarette. Dry your face. You know I speak like this in the tough love, as they say in English.'

Amir did as he was told and smoked one cigarette after the next, remembering his former wife and how Samir had never spoken like this when his marriage had fallen apart. If he had rolled around on the ground screaming, Samir would have dusted him off and hugged him with both arms.

He is right. He is all right.

Oh this pain, the pain of being alive.

He thanks Samir who waves him away. He leaves with clarity in his mind. Hold this clarity and do not let it escape and perhaps there will be a chance with her again.

STORYLINES

Years later you say to them: *Tell me how you met.*
　　They share a smile. It does not include you.

It was actually at a wedding.

　　　　　　　It was my family friend, her relative.

We were sitting at the same table.
He was off to one side.
She points in the general direction.

　　　　　　　Someone introduced us.
　　　Afterwards, I couldn't get her out of my mind.

You lie.
There were so many beautiful women that night,
everyone dressed up.
You didn't look too bad yourself.

He laughs.
You know it wasn't like that.
I only had eyes for you.

All those years ago . . .

All those years.

I think it's seventeen and a bit.

And two months.
It was July.

Yes it was.
And who knew where we'd end up?

I always thought we would be together,
that it would be for life.

Did you now?
How exactly did you know?

I just did.

But how?

You sense that long ago they have forgotten about you, that this is a memory, a story that contains only them, and if you're wise and you treasure your time, this is a cue for you to disappear.

SUBJECTS OF NOTE:
A catalogue

A catalogue of subjects that may have played a part and therefore deserve my thanks:

stars—navigation by said stars—history—world history—lots of history—local history—personal, impersonal and beyond personal history—science (botany, chemistry, biology, astronomy)—poets (Arabic, Persian, Russian, Spanish, Federico García Lorca especially)—Bolaño and Borges—sports such as football, rugby, football, tennis, football, actually just football—travels (past, present, futurepast)—differences between a plaza, square and park—behaviours peculiar to the magpie, red fish and alligator—naval systems and the *Titanic*—robot technologies—disputed territories and geopolitics—the word 'book' in various languages—falcons—music (opera and dance)—the colours red black white—poetry by Ibn Benito Almagro perhaps.